Meredith felt a finger touch lightly under her chin. She didn't resist...

Then, so softly she didn't realize it at first, Tom's hands were sliding against her cheeks, cradling her face.

"Look at me," he ordered, the tone soft but firm. She automatically raised her eyes to obey. And found herself looking straight into his. The breath caught in Meredith's throat. She peered, helplessly, into Tom's eyes, into his face, until everything else in the world seemed to fade away. There was nothing but the man in front of her, looking back at her.

He really did have the bluest eyes she'd ever seen. It seemed as though she could get lost in them forever, drifting in a sea of deep, bottomless blue. Yet it was more than the color that pulled her in. It was the kindness she saw in them, the empathy, the humanity.

The warmth of his hands on Meredith's cheeks, the softness of his skin, slowly sank into her system. Tom's gaze slowly lowered, drifting down her face. He focused there for an infinite moment, and Meredith suddenly had the feeling that he was about to kiss her...

KERRY CONNOR

THE BEST MAN TO TRUST

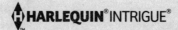
HARLEQUIN® INTRIGUE®

To everyone who's ever dreamed of the one that got away.

Recycling programs
for this product may
not exist in your area.

ISBN-13: 978-0-373-69696-3

THE BEST MAN TO TRUST

Copyright © 2013 by Kerry Connor

Printed in U.S.A.

www.Harlequin.com

ABOUT THE AUTHOR

A lifelong mystery reader, Kerry Connor first discovered romantic suspense by reading Harlequin Intrigue books and is thrilled to be writing for the line. Kerry lives and writes in New York.

Books by Kerry Connor

HARLEQUIN INTRIGUE
1067—STRANGERS IN THE NIGHT
1094—BEAUTIFUL STRANGER
1129—A STRANGER'S BABY
1170—TRUSTING A STRANGER
1207—STRANGER IN A SMALL TOWN
1236—SILENT NIGHT STAKEOUT
1268—CIRCUMSTANTIAL MARRIAGE
1334—HER COWBOY DEFENDER
1370—HER COWBOY AVENGER
1421—THE PERFECT BRIDE*
1429—THE BEST MAN TO TRUST*

*Sutton Hall Weddings

CAST OF CHARACTERS

Meredith Sutton—She was hoping for a fresh start—for herself and the mansion she'd inherited—only to find that history had a nasty way of repeating itself.

Tom Campbell—The best man was the only person Meredith could trust.

Rachel Delaney—The wedding of her dreams became everyone's worst nightmare.

Scott Pierce—The groom vowed to protect his bride.

Haley Nash—The maid of honor never expected what lay in store at her best friend's wedding.

Jessica Burke—The bridesmaid held a particular dislike of Meredith.

Greg Radford—The groomsman found comfort in the bottom of a bottle.

Alex Corbett—The reporter was dedicated to revealing the truth, but knew how to keep his own secrets.

Ellen Barnes—She was hired as Sutton Hall's new cook, but found herself dealing with far more than she'd signed on for.

Rick Tucker—The handyman was an outsider—and an enigma.

Chapter One

The storm was getting worse.

Meredith Sutton stood in the open doorway and watched the darkness gathering over Sutton Hall. The snow had been coming down for a several hours now, but it was only in the past couple that it had become clear just how bad this storm would be. The wind had picked up, shaking the windows and whistling through the eaves. Light flurries had turned into a heavy downfall, as though a white curtain had been dropped over the world. The curtain was still translucent, but soon it would be impenetrable.

Staring out into the snow, Meredith tried to convince herself that the feeling of unease weighing down on her was solely due to the weather.

Unfortunately, lying to herself wasn't that easy. As she kept an eye on the end of the driveway, she was entirely too aware of the cause of her apprehension.

They should have been here by now. If they didn't arrive soon, they might not arrive at all. They might be forced to stay in town, or at the airport.

Which might not be such a bad thing, a voice whispered in the back of her mind.

Meredith did her best to shake off the doubts. Nothing was going to happen this weekend. The wedding would go perfectly.

She would never make it through the next few days if she let herself think otherwise.

"Any sign of them yet?"

The voice came from behind her, just before Rick Tucker, the new handyman at Sutton Hall, appeared beside her to stick his head outside and look for himself.

"Not yet," Meredith said.

"They should be here by now," Rick murmured. "Hope they didn't get stuck in town."

"Hmm," Meredith replied, unable to bring herself to agree. "If they were smart they wouldn't try to make it up the mountain in this weather."

"I guess so. Shame if the wedding was canceled, though. It'll be nice to get the first wedding under our belts, won't it? Finally get a fresh start for this place."

"Yes, it will." Funny, but when she'd come here, *she* was supposed be the one getting a fresh start. She'd never dreamed the place itself would need one, never imagined the terrible things that would happen here.

It had been a year and a half since she and her brother, Adam, inherited Sutton Hall, an elegant manor in the mountains of Vermont, from a distant relative they'd never heard of. A year and a half since she had taken one look at the high ceilings and gorgeous wooden interiors, the mountain views and garden outside, and decided this would be a beautiful place to hold weddings. A year and a half since she'd begun work on the business that was supposed to be her new beginning.

And six months since the first bride to come to Sutton Hall had been murdered, thrown off the balcony of the bridal suite.

The killer had eventually been caught, but most of the couples whose weddings had been scheduled after that first one that never took place had understandably canceled. Meredith had returned their deposits though she hadn't legally been required to, not really blaming them for the decision. A dozen weddings had been booked before the murder, and all had canceled.

All but one.

During the flurry of cancellations, Meredith had fully expected the Delaney/Pierce wedding to follow suit. When that hadn't happened, Meredith had called Rachel Delaney to confirm she hadn't simply forgotten to do so, or to make sure she'd heard about what had happened here. But no, Rachel had verified that she knew about the murder and she and her groom still wanted to be married at Sutton Hall. Everything was to proceed as planned.

Of course the one wedding that wasn't canceled was the one Meredith had been dreading from the start.

Unlike the other couples who'd originally planned to have their weddings here, Rachel Delaney and Scott Pierce weren't strangers to her. Not entirely, at least. The three of them had gone to the same college and graduated together seven years ago. Meredith hadn't really known Scott, and she and Rachel had only been acquaintances at best, but there was enough of a connection that they weren't completely unfamiliar with each other, although she hadn't seen either of them since college. Meredith had recognized a few of the other names on the guest list, all of them fellow alumni.

It was a time Meredith wasn't particularly fond of remembering. Unfortunately, there wasn't going to be much chance of avoiding it this weekend.

Adam and his fiancée, Jillian, were supposed to be here to help her with this, but they'd taken what was supposed to be a short trip to San Francisco so Jillian could take care of some business, only to find themselves stuck there longer than they'd intended. First Jillian had come down with a stomach virus and they'd missed their original flight, then their replacement flight had been canceled due to the storm. The flight she'd wanted to arrive hadn't and the one she'd been worried about coming had.

She could only hope it wasn't a sign of how her luck was going to go this weekend.

Twin beams of light suddenly materialized through the curtain of snow, aiming dimly at her. She immediately recognized it as an approaching vehicle, relief and dread surging inside her. She couldn't tell which was stronger.

She watched as the vehicle gradually took shape through the snow, emerging as a passenger car. Another car soon appeared behind it. They slowly rounded the circular driveway in front of the house, pulling up a few yards from the door where she waited.

The first car had barely pulled to a stop when Rick brushed by her, hurrying out to help the newcomers. She belatedly realized she should do the same. She'd been holding her coat in front of her the whole time, the item dangling loosely from her hands.

By the time she started to shrug into it, the passenger doors were opening and a few bundled-up figures began dashing toward her through the snow.

Tossing her coat aside, Meredith pulled the door open farther to let the newcomers in. Seconds later, they reached the front stoop and hurried over the threshold.

They came to a stop in front of her, immediately stomping the snow from their boots. She waited as they started to shed their heavy layers, unraveling scarves, pushing back hoods and tugging off gloves.

They were all women, Meredith saw. She instantly recognized the one closest to her, even before the woman opened her mouth and said, "Meredith?" in a voice she'd heard numerous times over the phone the past few weeks. This was Rachel Delaney, the bride-to-be.

"Rachel," she said with a smile. "It's great to see you. Welcome to Sutton Hall."

"Thank you. I can't believe we made it!"

"Honestly, I can't believe you tried! I was sure you would have decided to ride out the storm somewhere." *And probably should have,* she thought, as a strong gust of wind burst through the still-open door, blowing snow in at them.

A slim brunette with dark brown eyes, Rachel laughed, her face aglow. "Are you kidding? I wasn't going to let anything keep me from my wedding." Her eyes finally moved past Meredith, widening as they took in the massive front entryway of Sutton Hall. "Or this place. My God, it's even more amazing than I'd imagined."

Meredith swallowed a sigh of relief at the pleasure in the woman's voice. Rachel had been very particular about every aspect of the arrangements so far. An interior decorator by profession, she had an eye for design and, as she'd made clear over the past few months, she knew what she wanted. Meredith had been bracing herself to deal with a very high-maintenance bride on top of everything else. It was good to know one thing had met with her approval. Hopefully it meant they would get the weekend off on the right foot, the weather notwithstanding.

In spite of everything, Meredith couldn't help but feel a twinge of pride as she turned to follow Rachel's gaze. Sutton Hall's front foyer certainly made an incredible first impression. The vast entrance hall stretched two stories high. An elaborate crystal chandelier hung from the ceiling, and below it a plush red carpet led the way across the marble floor to the staircase at the other end. The grand staircase split into two halfway up and continued curving up to the second floor in opposite directions. Even after more than a year here, the sight of this room never failed to amaze her.

"Oh!" Rachel exclaimed, drawing Meredith's attention back to her. "I'm sorry, I'm being rude. I should introduce you, if you don't know each other already." She motioned toward the other women. "Meredith, these are my bridesmaids and two of my oldest friends in the world, Haley Nash and Jessica Burke. Guys, this is Meredith Sutton."

Haley Nash, Meredith knew, was the maid of honor. A tall, lean blonde, she greeted Meredith with a smile. Her face was open and friendly, but Meredith still felt herself shrink a little inside reflexively. The woman had the kind of beauty that had always made her feel inadequate, as though she shouldn't be standing anywhere near this person. She did her best to hide it, pasting on a smile and meeting Haley's eyes long enough to not seem rude.

Jessica Burke was also beautiful, but that wasn't what Meredith immediately noticed about her. It was the hostility glittering in the woman's dark eyes as she stared back at Meredith, her lips compressed in a thinly concealed frown. Meredith barely managed to keep from frowning herself. She didn't remember Jessica well from school, was pretty sure they'd never said two words to each other. She couldn't imagine what the woman would have against her.

Before she could figure it out, several more figures suddenly burst through the doorway. Meredith quickly took stock of the newcomers as they began casting off layers like the women had. She recognized Alex Corbett, having worked with him on the school paper back in college. He'd gone on to become a respected journalist, making quite a name for himself as an investigative reporter. He was going to be officiating the ceremony. The man beside him had to be Greg Radford, she guessed, remembering the name of the best man from the guest list. The man behind them pulled off the scarf covering his face, revealing Scott Pierce, Rachel's fiancée, a tall man with dark hair and eyes.

But it wasn't the groom-to-be who grabbed her attention.

It was the man behind him, brushing snow from the hair that was as blond and thick as the last time she'd seen it. Everything inside her went utterly still.

Tom Campbell.

Recognition slammed into her like a blow to the chest. His was a name, a face she hadn't thought of in years, had actually forgotten somehow. As soon as she realized that fact it seemed impossible to believe.

In an instant, she was eighteen again, staring across a crowded room at the most beautiful boy she'd ever seen in her whole life, everything within her freezing as it did now.

How many times had she stood exactly like this, staring at him, unable to look away….

Desperately hoping he'd notice her.

Terrified that he would, not wanting to see the look on his face when someone that beautiful cast his eyes on her.

He hadn't noticed her, of course. Then, or ever. Why would he? He was beautiful. And she was…

Her.

No, when someone had finally noticed her, it had been Brad.

And her nightmare had begun.

Meredith tried to shake the onslaught of memories even as the emotions they raised threatened to rack her body. She didn't have time to go down that path. Not now. Not ever, really.

She'd just begun to get a grip on her emotions when Tom Campbell suddenly raised his head.

For the first time, his eyes met hers. And her heart suddenly, stupidly, stopped dead in her chest.

He was somehow even better-looking than he'd been before. But of course, he'd only been a boy then, all of eighteen or nineteen. The years had added maturity to his face, deepening its character, wiping away all traces of boyishness. The face before her was a man's, his jaw strong, his features lean and chiseled. The eyes were the same, though, still a deep, startling blue, the color so rich it seemed she could lose herself in them if she looked long enough.

His lips curved upward slightly in a polite but vague smile, as if she was a stranger.

Which she was to him, of course.

"Oh, I'm sorry!" Rachel suddenly said, jolting Meredith's attention away from the man who'd held it so fully. Meredith realized she'd probably been staring. Oh, God, she hoped she hadn't been staring....

Grimacing apologetically, Rachel gestured toward Tom. "Meredith, I hope it's not a problem, but there's a small change in plans. This is Tom Campbell, Scott's best man."

Meredith didn't have to fake her surprise. "Oh, I thought— His name wasn't on the guest list...."

"Campbell was my first choice, but he originally couldn't make the date, so Radford was going to stand in," Scott explained with a nod toward the third man who stood a few feet away. "But at the last minute Campbell was able to make it after all."

"I'm sorry I didn't get a chance to let you know beforehand that there'd be an extra guest," Rachel said. "It really was last-minute and I had so many other things to keep track of...."

"I hope it won't be an imposition," Tom said, his voice so warm and deep she felt it roll along her skin and nearly shuddered.

She managed to meet the bluest eyes she'd ever seen without wavering. "Of course not," she said, her voice thankfully steady. "Obviously we have plenty of room."

She waved a hand toward the cavernous space around them to emphasize the point.

As she did, the lights chose that particular moment to flicker once, then twice, before steadying, as though to demonstrate the precariousness of the power. "Now we just need electricity," she said with a chuckle, deliberately keeping her tone light in response to the nervousness that passed across her guests' faces. "Fortunately, we have a generator if the power goes out. We'll be fine."

The anxiety gradually faded from their expressions, exactly as she'd intended. Fortunately she had plenty of experience trying to appease disgruntled moods. With any luck she wouldn't have to rely on it too much over the next few days.

Five days, she thought faintly. Today was Thursday. They were scheduled to leave Monday. They would be here for five days.

Tom Campbell would be here for five days.

Behind the group, Rick hurried into the entryway with a few bags, closing the door behind him. Everyone must be accounted for. "Now then," Meredith said. "Why don't we show you to your rooms so you can get settled in? We can take care of your bags later. Our cook is working on dinner as we speak, so I hope you're all hungry."

The statement was met with a chorus of cheers and excited chatter, confirming she'd managed to put her guests back in a good mood. As she turned toward the stairs to lead the way up, she felt her own tension ease the slightest bit.

Everything's going to be fine, she told herself again.

She just hoped there wouldn't be any more surprises this weekend.

"What do you think?"

Tom Campbell tilted his head back and surveyed the

high ceiling and ornate chandelier suspended overhead. "It's really something," he said, knowing it had to be the understatement of the year.

"That it is," Scott said with a chuckle. "Bet you're glad you brought a camera with you, aren't you?"

Tom forced a chuckle of his own. "Something like that."

"Who knows? Maybe you could use some place like this for a new show."

"Maybe." Tom kept his eyes up, resisting the impulse to clench his jaw. He was no stranger to having people pitch ideas for shows to him. Once they found out he worked in television, they inevitably wanted to share the great idea they'd always had for a series. But he knew Scott wasn't trying to sell his own idea. His old friend was trying to be helpful, supportive. Instead, all he was doing was reminding Tom of the fact that he was currently unemployed.

He knew he was luckier than a lot of people. He'd gotten to spend six years doing his dream job, which was more than many people could say in their entire lifetimes. As an on-site producer and cameraman for *On the Wild Side,* a reality/documentary series that traveled to some of the most spectacular and remotest places on earth, he'd gotten to see and experience things most people never would. But just as they'd been preparing to leave to shoot the new season, the network had informed them they'd been canceled.

He'd known there was a chance it was coming. The signs were there. But they'd already been renewed, and at the very least he'd thought they'd be able to complete one final season. They'd been ready to go out with a bang. Instead, the journey had come to an abrupt end.

One of the lone upsides of his sudden unemployment was that he'd been able to make Scott's wedding after all. And it brought him to an entirely different kind of spectacular and remote place.

Tom had gotten to see some amazing locales, but he'd certainly never seen anything like Sutton Hall, at least not in person. He hadn't been able to get much of an impression of the outside of the building through the snow—only enough to tell that it was massive, the immense stone structure towering several stories high and seeming to stretch the full length of the mountain it sat upon. But the inside was even more incredible, far more elegant and lavish than any hotel he'd ever been in. It was so impressive it was almost possible to forget what had happened here so recently.

Almost.

"And it really doesn't make you nervous getting married here?" he had to ask.

"I'm trying not to think about…all of that," Scott admitted. "The only thing I care about is marrying Rachel. This is what she wants, and as long as I can do it for her, I will."

Tom wasn't surprised. Rachel had always been someone who wanted her own way, and Scott had always been willing to go along with whatever she wanted. Scott also hadn't grown up with much money, and Tom knew the fact that he could afford to give Rachel this wedding had to be a point of pride for him.

No, the surprising part was that the wedding was taking place at all. "I still sort of can't believe you guys are really getting married after all this time."

Scott laughed. "Honestly, sometimes I can't believe it, either. What can I say? I guess it was just meant to be."

Maybe it was, Tom agreed silently. Scott and Rachel had been a couple for more than two years in college before breaking up senior year for reasons that had never entirely clear to Tom. Last year they'd run into each other again, discovering they were both still single and the connection was still there between them. Whatever had happened in the past, they appeared to have put it behind them and were now stronger than ever. And now here they were, ready to get married. It was a reassuring example that maybe things did work out sometimes in this crazy world after all.

Of course, first the wedding had to go off without a hitch. Judging by some of the comments from the rest of the wedding party since they'd met up at the airport, he wasn't the only one wondering if Scott and Rachel weren't tempting fate by deciding to come here for their nuptials.

It wasn't only the wedding party that was slightly on edge. Tom hadn't missed the tension on Meredith Sutton's face beneath her carefully constructed good cheer. Her smile had never wavered, but it was there in the tightness of that smile, the way her expression was so thoroughly locked into place, as though she refused to let anyone see anything other than what she wanted them to.

She was nervous, and was doing everything she could not to show it.

He doubted the others would notice it. Too bad he was just a little too good at reading faces. And he couldn't help but feel a flicker of unease in the pit of his gut in response.

Considering what had happened here before, Meredith Sutton probably had good reason to be nervous. He just had to wonder if that was the only reason.

He watched her start up the stairs at the other end of the space, leading the group that trailed behind her. She was thin—maybe too much so—her posture ramrod straight, her shoulder-length brown hair floating behind her slightly as she walked. She made a strangely vulnerable picture, dwarfed by the size of the space around her.

The lights suddenly flickered again, drawing his attention back to the chandelier.

"Come on," Scott said, clapping him on the back. "We don't want to get left behind."

"Especially if the lights do go out," he agreed. Picking up his bags, he gave one more glance around the lush hall. He had to admit, this would be an amazing place for a wedding. His professional instincts kicking in, he could easily envision it, picturing the shots, the perfect angles to capture it all. Everyone might be a little uneasy now, but if everything went well, it would all be worth it.

When everything went well, he corrected himself, moving to follow Scott to the stairs. They were all being ridiculous. Nothing was going to happen this weekend. Nothing but the wedding of Scott and Rachel's dreams.

SUTTON HALL CERTAINLY lived up to its reputation. It was beautiful, classical, extravagant.

And creepy.

It was partly due to the weather, as the lights flickered again, each flash seeming to indicate the power could go out at any moment, plunging them into darkness.

But it was more than that. No matter how stunning the surroundings were, it was impossible to forget that someone had died here only six months ago, that a murderer had once walked these halls.

Just as another one did now.

Cool eyes watched as a few members of the group shuddered while they made their way up the stairs. They were nervous.

They should be. They just didn't know how true that was.

But they would. Soon.

A place like this, which had so recently served as the backdrop for death, was the perfect setting for a few more.

Anyone would be a fool to come to a place like this for a wedding.

And fools like that deserved whatever happened to them here.

Chapter Two

Even before she pushed through the kitchen door and stepped into the room, Meredith was greeted by incredible aromas that immediately had her mouth watering. Based on the smells she was creating, Sutton Hall's new cook, Ellen Barnes, had dinner well in hand. Meredith nearly let out a sigh of relief. At least one thing was going right so far this weekend.

The cook was working at the kitchen island across from the oven as Meredith entered. A full-figured woman in her forties with reddish-blond hair, she looked up with a smile, the sight of her open, friendly face instantly lightening Meredith's mood. "Everyone settled in all right?"

"I think so," Meredith said. Okay, so that was another thing that had gone well enough. Everyone seemed pleased with the rooms she'd given them. Even the few who'd looked a little uneasy about being here appeared to have been won over when they saw the accommodations, she thought with a touch of pride. Score one for Sutton Hall. "Rick's helping them with their luggage. I'm going to go do the same but I thought I'd make sure everything was okay in here."

"Yep, everything's almost ready," Ellen said with a satisfied nod. "I hope your guests are ready to eat."

"Based on how they reacted when I mentioned dinner,

I'd say they are. Should I tell them we'll be ready to serve in a half an hour?"

"Sounds about right."

"I'll be back to help serve. Unless you need me to do anything now…?"

"Nope. I've got it all under control."

Meredith couldn't argue with her there. Everything looked as amazing as it smelled.

Not for the first time, she thought how lucky they'd been to find the woman. When they'd had to replace the original staff following the terrible events of a few months ago, she'd had her doubts about whether they'd be able to find anyone good. They couldn't promise long-term employment at the moment. They didn't know if they'd be able to keep the business—or Sutton Hall—going much longer. A lot depended on how the wedding went this weekend, if they could get some good publicity. Until they had a better idea of what the future held, they couldn't hire a full-time staff.

That left them trying to find locals willing to work on a part-time or temporary basis for the time being. It hadn't been easy. After the murder, many locals hadn't wanted anything to do with the place. Luckily she'd found Ellen and Rick, both of whom lived in the area and had surpassed her wildest expectations.

Good thing, too. It looked like it was going to be just the three of them this weekend. While the rest of the temporary staff she'd hired had planned to drive in during the day, Rick and Ellen had both agreed to stay at Sutton Hall through the weekend even before they'd known about the storm.

"Thanks again for being willing to stay this weekend," Meredith said.

Ellen waved off the comment with a flutter of her hand. "Doesn't look like I'd be able to go anywhere if I wanted to."

Meredith turned toward the windows, unable to see anything through the glass but a cloud of white. "You're probably right about that." The snow wasn't supposed to stop until tomorrow evening at the earliest, with the worst yet to come tonight. No one would be getting out of here for a few days at least. They were well and truly stuck, she thought with a flicker of trepidation.

Once again, the wish that Adam and Jillian were here floated through her mind. This time she did her best to shake off the feeling. She was the one who'd wanted to open Sutton Hall for weddings. Part of that had been wanting to prove to everyone—and herself—that she was capable of running this business, that she was strong enough. With Adam and Jillian gone, this was truly it, a chance to stand on her own two feet.

The idea strengthened her resolve and she pushed away the last of her doubts.

Whatever challenges lay ahead this weekend, she'd have to handle them herself.

THE SOUND OF SILVERWARE clinking against glass cut through the light buzz of conversation in the dining room, silencing the group.

Tom looked up in time to see Greg rising to his feet, glass firmly in hand. "I'd like to make a toast," he announced. "After all, this is a party, even if no one's acting like it."

A few muted chuckles greeted his comment, which was entirely too accurate. The mood in the room had been subdued ever since they'd sat down to dinner.

The rooms Meredith had led them to were all beautifully furnished and more than comfortable. The problem wasn't with the rooms. None of them were getting cell phone reception. Whether it was due to the weather or the location—or both—wasn't clear, but it only emphasized the fact that they were cut off out here. Isolated. Trapped.

Everyone was trying to put on a brave face, no one wanting to put a damper on Scott and Rachel's weekend, but the tension in the room was unmistakable.

Greg turned toward Scott and Rachel, who sat together on one side of the table, and raised his glass. From the way he weaved slightly on his feet, he'd already had a few drinks.

"To Scott and Rachel," he declared with a broad smile. "Finally together again, soon to officially be together forever. Happy wedding to you."

"Hear! Hear!" Alex chimed in.

Everyone raised their glasses and, with a collective "cheers," took a drink.

Over the rim of his glass, Tom watched Greg retake his seat, his hand unsteady as he reached for the chair. Greg had always been a big man, stocky rather than fat, though he seemed a little thicker around the middle. Other than the possible weight gain, Tom noted with a pang of discomfort that Greg evidently hadn't changed much. He'd always been the life of every party, always drinking too much. In the heady days of freshman year when they'd all been on their own for the first time, his behavior had seemed fun and exciting, but by senior year it had gotten old. These many years later, it seemed even sadder.

Still, maybe he was being too hard on him, Tom acknowledged. Greg was a real estate broker and, based on the way he was dressed, a successful one. Presumably he didn't drink like this all the time. And Greg was right, this *was* supposed to be a party. Not to mention more than a few of the others had wasted no time hitting the wine once they'd sat down for dinner. It probably wasn't a surprise given the circumstances.

"Thank you everyone for coming all this way," Scott said. "I know I speak for Rachel as well as myself when I say we're so glad to have you here to share this occasion with us. You were there when we first met and were to-gether. It's only right that you be here to share this next step on our journey with us."

"We wouldn't have missed it for anything," Haley said. A few others murmured their agreement.

Tom silently studied the faces gathered around the table, these people who were both so familiar and so unknown to him at the same time. It felt strange being around them for the first time in so many years, like stepping back into another life, one that didn't even feel like it used to be his.

They all seemed to have done well for themselves. His and Haley's flights had arrived before everyone else's, so they'd had some time to talk at the airport before everyone else had arrived. She seemed to have a thriving career in public relations. Alex was a highly respected investigative reporter who'd already won several awards for his work. Jess was an actress who'd found some acclaim in Chicago's renowned theater scene. Rachel was the owner of her own interior design firm. And of course, Scott's career as an investment banker had allowed them to afford this wedding in the first place.

Only then did he remember that one face he would have expected to see here wasn't. "What about Kim?" he asked. Kim Logan had been one of Rachel's closest friends back in school. The two of them, plus Haley and Jessica, had been inseparable. "Couldn't she make it?"

An awkward silence fell over the table, and he immediately knew he'd said something wrong.

Scott finally cleared his throat. "I forgot you probably hadn't heard," he said quietly. "Kim died a couple months ago."

Shock jolted through him. Kim had to have been around

twenty-nine or thirty like the rest of them, far too young for anyone to die. "What happened?"

"She drowned in her bathtub," Haley said. "She'd taken too many pills and fell asleep in the tub. She probably didn't even have a chance to save herself."

"So it wasn't a suicide?"

Haley shook her head. "Accidental overdose."

Tom remembered how much Kim had loved to drink, and he'd suspected she'd consumed the occasional recreational drug now and then. She and Greg had been the wild ones in the group, the ones who'd always had a little too much fun. Evidently she'd only gotten worse over the years.

If Greg had learned anything from their friend's death, he didn't show it. As Tom watched, he pulled out a flask and unscrewed the top, taking a long pull from it.

"I'm sorry to hear that," Tom said.

"Not that she would have been invited anyway," Jessica murmured under her breath, so low Tom was sure he was the only one who'd heard the comment.

He glanced at Jessica, only to find her staring into her wineglass.

"It's just a reminder that we never know what's going to happen," Scott said. He reached out and took Rachel's hand. "And how we have to live every moment to the fullest."

"Exactly," Haley said with a smile. "And that's what we should be celebrating this weekend—the two of you starting a new life together."

"Maybe in more ways than one." Alex grinned. "How about it, you two? Any plans to start a family anytime soon?"

Scott matched his grin. "We can't wait to have kids." He looked at Rachel, his face practically glowing with love for her. "Right, honey?"

"Right," Rachel said automatically, matching his smile.

Watching her, Tom felt a twinge of unease as he took in her expression. Her smile seemed strained, the single word somehow forced…

If there was anything off about her response, Scott didn't seem to notice it. His face still beaming, he leaned in to kiss her. Her own smile deepening, Rachel accepted the kiss with unmistakable happiness, her eyes drifting shut as their lips met.

Tom nearly shook himself. He must have imagined whatever it was he thought he'd noticed. Scott was certainly much more familiar with Rachel's expressions than he was, and if he hadn't detected anything off about it, then there probably hadn't been.

The door to the kitchen suddenly swung open, cutting off the rest of his thoughts. A moment later, Meredith stepped through the entryway, carrying a tray. The cook—Ellen, she'd said her name was—followed close behind, pushing a cart.

"I hope you're ready for the main course," Meredith announced.

"That smells incredible," Rachel said. "What is it?"

"I made a roast," Ellen said. The comment was immediately greeted with murmurs of excitement. Tom had to concur. The food smelled better than anything he'd had in a long time.

As Ellen placed the roast on the table, Meredith began to move around, collecting the salad plates. Tom watched her work, looking for any signs of the same tension he'd detected earlier. If she felt any, she was doing a better job of hiding it. The smile was still fixed on her face, but it seemed less forced. Even so, he noticed that she never looked directly at anyone, keeping her attention on the table and plates.

She's uncomfortable around us, he realized. He wondered if her reaction was related to the murder or if it was them specifically who triggered her uneasiness, and if so, why that would be.

Wondered why he was analyzing the woman's movements so closely when she was just trying to do her job. Wondered what it was about her he found so fascinating.

"Meredith," Jessica said suddenly. "I was sorry to hear about you and Brad."

His focus on her, Tom didn't miss the sudden tightness that gripped Meredith's features, her shoulders stiffening almost defensively.

She mustered a polite smile. "Thank you."

"Divorces can be so rough. So much…*unpleasantness,* so many things being said."

"That's very true," Meredith murmured, her eyes downcast. "If you'll excuse me…" Without waiting for a response, she quickly turned and walked back into the kitchen.

An uncomfortable silence fell in her wake. "What was that about?" Scott asked.

"Do you remember Brad Jackson from college?" Jessica said. "She's his ex-wife. Divorced him a couple years ago. He wanted to work things out, so she made up some stories that he used to beat her to get out of the marriage."

"Are you sure they were stories?" Haley asked softly.

"Of course they were," Jessica scoffed. "You remember Brad. He would never do anything like that. She was lying to get more money out of him."

Alex cast a glance around the room. "I have to say, Jess, from the looks of this place, she doesn't need the money."

"This was *before* she inherited this place," Jessica said.

No one had a response to that, everyone seeming to return their attention to their food simultaneously.

Frowning, Tom tried to remember Brad Jackson and managed to come up with a vague image, but nothing concrete. The name was barely familiar. He doubted he'd known the guy very well.

However, he had no trouble remembering Meredith's reaction to the mention of her ex-husband. And everything about her response said she hadn't been lying in the divorce.

Sympathy tugged hard in the pit of his stomach. God, what she must have gone through. He tried to imagine anyone hurting the vulnerable woman who'd just ducked out of the room. The idea was unspeakable.

Glancing at Jess, he studied the smug expression on her face. At the airport, she'd tried chatting him up a bit. He'd suspected it was because she'd thought he might have some connections in the entertainment industry to help her with her acting career. She'd come on so strong he couldn't help but be put off by her. That was nothing compared to his reaction to her now. He wondered if she'd changed over the years, or if she'd always been this unlikable and he'd simply never noticed. They'd never been close—she'd been Rachel's friend, not his or Scott's—but he couldn't remember ever being this repulsed by her.

Hiding a grimace to keep anyone from noticing his reaction, Tom turned his attention back to his plate.

He was starting to get the feeling this weekend couldn't be over soon enough.

BY MIDNIGHT, SUTTON HALL was quiet and still. Everyone had retreated to their own rooms long ago. The corridors were heavy with shadows and silence. Most were likely in bed by now.

But not everyone.

One of the doors along the corridor slowly opened. Cold eyes surveyed the empty hallway. Once satisfied, the watcher slipped through the doorway, a smile sliding into place.

Showtime.

Chapter Three

Midnight, Meredith noted, studying the clock on the stove. She really should go to bed, even though she knew there was no chance of her falling asleep anytime soon.

She sat alone in the mammoth kitchen of Sutton Hall, perched on a stool at the center island, nursing a cup of hot chocolate that was starting to turn cold. Only the row of lights above the island was on, leaving the rest of the room under cover of darkness.

It should have been unsettling, sitting in the massive room surrounded by shadows, the silence echoing around her. It made her feel utterly alone. At the moment, that seemed more comforting than threatening. She'd had enough of people for one day, and nothing that lurked in the darkness could be as dangerous as what was in her own head.

She'd known this weekend would inevitably bring up some memories. She'd even thought someone might mention Brad, might know about the divorce. But somehow she hadn't expected anyone would know how terrible their marriage had been—or would bring it up so deliberately.

Most days she didn't even think about him, and considered herself lucky that was the case. But Jessica Burke's comments had ripped the lid off that tiny box in the back of her mind where she usually managed to keep her memo ories locked up tight. No matter how hard she tried, she couldn't seem to get that lid back on. There was no avoiding the memories, no blocking out the things she wished she could forget.

The way his face looked, both beaming with love…and twisted with hatred.

The sound of his voice, roaring with contempt and rage.

The words he used to fling at her, hitting right at every deep-seated fear and insecurity, the ones she still heard sometimes in her dreams.

You're worthless. You're nothing.

His words hadn't hurt her. How could they? He hadn't been telling her anything she didn't already know.

No, his words hadn't hurt her. He'd had to use his fists for that.

And so he had.

The door to the dining room suddenly sprang into motion, jolting her out of her thoughts. Meredith shot upright in her seat, her heart jumping, as the door slowly swung open.

Seconds later, Tom Campbell stepped through the entryway and into the room.

As it always seemed to, everything inside her went still for a moment as she breathed in the sight of him. Even in the dim lighting of the room, there was no mistaking how good-looking he was, the faint glow catching every perfect angle on his face, his hair still gleaming and golden.

Stop it, she told herself as her heart finally kicked back into motion, beating harder and faster than before. It was pathetic. Ten years after the first time she'd seen him, and she was still struck dumb by the sight of the man, still that pitiful girl hoping a boy like that would notice her when he never had.

This time he did see her, though, his eyes falling on her an instant later and widening in surprise.

And damned if something inside her didn't melt just a little bit in response.

"Oh," he said, his lips curving in a wry smile. "I wasn't expecting to find anyone in here."

A small chuckle worked its way from her lungs. "I wasn't expecting company, either, so I guess that makes two of us."

"I'm sorry," he said, his voice softening with genuine concern. "I didn't mean to scare you."

"You didn't," she lied. "Did you need something?"

"I couldn't sleep, so I thought I might try to get a snack or something. I hope that's all right..."

"Of course," Meredith said with her best hostess smile, rising from her seat. "The kitchen is always open to guests, and we make sure to keep some cold cuts and other snacks on hand in the fridge. I think there's some cake left over from dinner and some cookies, too. What can I get you?"

"Actually, whatever it is you're drinking smells great."

"It's just hot chocolate."

"I wouldn't say no to that. I can make it myself if you tell me where—"

"No, no," she said, waving him toward the kitchen island. "You're a guest here. It's no trouble."

Meredith quickly moved to the counter for a mug. Behind her, she heard him pull a stool out from the island to take a seat.

"So," he said. "Are you here because you're really that dedicated to serving your guests, or couldn't you sleep, either?"

"I wish I could say it's the first one, but I have to admit, I have a lot on my mind." Wanting to dodge any question of what it might be that was keeping her up, she went for the obvious one. "I'm sure you heard about what happened to our first wedding here."

"The murdered bride. I'm surprised you wanted to have any more weddings here after that."

"I wasn't sure I did," Meredith said. "I was surprised Rachel wanted to go ahead with having hers, but as long as she did I couldn't say no."

"When it goes well, maybe it'll give this place a clean slate."

She didn't miss the fact that he said "when" the wedding went well, not "if." She had to appreciate his confidence, or at least that he was capable of such positive thinking. "I hope so," she agreed. "What about you? What's keeping you up?"

"Guess I'm just trying to process everything that happened today, how different everybody is. It feels a little strange being around everyone after all this time."

"You didn't keep in touch with any of them over the years?"

"Not really. Only Scott, and then we'd only talk every once in a while, grab a drink when I was in town. After we graduated, I got caught up in work and sort of lost touch with everybody else."

"I think someone said you work in television?"

"I'm a cameraman and on-site producer for a show called *On the Wild Side*." He paused. "At least I was. The show was just canceled. You'd think I'd be used to it by now but I guess it's still too new."

"I'm sorry," she said. "That's why you were able to make it to the wedding after all?"

"Yeah. I guess that's one good thing to come out of it."

His hot chocolate finally prepared, Meredith turned back to face him, setting the mug in front of him. "Here you go."

"Thanks." Reaching for the mug, he looked up and met her eyes. His gaze was unexpectedly serious, and her skin tingled under the force of his attention. "I'm sorry about your marriage."

Meredith wasn't sure which was more surprising, the words themselves or the genuine emotion in his voice as he said them. She ignored the painful twinge in her chest at the memory and forced a smile. "Thank you."

"I didn't really know Brad in college."

Me, either, she thought grimly. She hadn't gotten to know who he really was until much later. "You didn't miss out on much." Realizing she might be opening the door to more questions she didn't want to answer, she gave her head a quick shake. "What about you? Been down the aisle yourself?"

He smiled ruefully. "No. Between traveling so much for work and never meeting anyone who's made me even consider it, I haven't come anywhere close."

"Maybe that's what's keeping you up," she suggested lightly. "All this talk about the wedding and impending marriage can't be much fun for a single guy."

He chuckled. "I don't have any aversion to marriage. My parents have a great one. I definitely want to get married someday. I just have to find the right woman."

"I'm sure you will," she said, having trouble believing he hadn't already.

He shrugged one shoulder carelessly. "I hope you're right."

As he took a sip from his cup, Meredith couldn't help smiling to herself. Never in a million years would she ever have expected to be talking to Tom Campbell, under any circumstances, let alone late at night, in the massive kitchen of a nineteenth-century mansion she'd inherited.

Just another example of how life really doesn't happen the way you expect it, she thought, nearly shaking her head in amazement.

And somehow he'd managed to live up to every fantasy she'd once had of him. Deep down she'd had this fear that he was actually a jerk. No one that good-looking could be a nice guy, could he? Yet here he was, even better-looking than she remembered, even nicer than she'd ever dreamed, talking to her, of all people.

She watched him tilt his head back, draining the last of the hot chocolate from his mug, his Adam's apple bobbing as he swallowed.

He lowered the cup to the counter with a soft sigh of satisfaction. "I think that was exactly what I needed."

"Time for bed then?" she asked. Only after the words came out did she realize how they might have sounded.

If he detected any innuendo in them, he didn't show it, simply returning her smile. The warmth on that impossibly handsome face sent a fresh wave of heat rushing through her. "I think so. You?"

She nodded. "I should. I have an early day tomorrow." Actually, it already was tomorrow, she realized. She'd be lucky to get a few hours of sleep.

Taking his cup, Meredith placed both mugs in the sink, then moved to the door where he waited, shutting off the lights behind her.

Together they made their way through the dining room and into the main hall.

"It was nice talking to you," Tom said as they reached the staircase.

"You, too," she said, and smiled, warmth spilling through her chest.

He opened his mouth to say something else.

He didn't get the chance.

A sound suddenly sliced through the stillness, cutting off whatever he'd been about to say. Loud. Shrill.

A scream.

Meredith shot a glance at Tom, their eyes meeting for a split second, the surprise in his matching her own, just before another scream reached them, then another.

It was a woman, screaming over and over again, each shriek louder and more filled with terror than the last.

They bolted in unison for the stairs. Her heart in her throat, Meredith took them two at a time, Tom right by her side. All the while it felt like she was moving too slow, the screams ringing over and over.

She finally reached the second floor, rounding the corner to peer down the hall.

A woman stood in the middle of the hallway, her back to them. It was Jessica, Meredith recognized, taking in the woman's height and the color of her hair. She was the one who was screaming.

Meredith instantly picked up a burst of speed, hurrying toward the woman. "Jessica?"

The woman didn't react to the sound of her name, her screams going on and on. "Jessica! What is it? What's wrong?"

No response. Meredith reached out, ready to grab the woman's shoulder, anything to get her attention, when her gaze fell past Jessica to the floor in front of her.

Shock ripped through her. Meredith missed a step and stumbled, pitching forward. An instant later, she felt a hand close around her elbow, steadying her. *Tom,* she recognized instinctively. The knowledge barely penetrated, every bit of her brainpower focused on the sight in front of her, on trying to make sense of it, on trying to absorb the horror that surged from her gut and rose in her throat.

No. It can't be. It can't—

But it was. No matter how many times she blinked, the sight refused to go away.

Haley lay in the middle of the hallway, her eyes staring upward, a knife sticking out of her chest.

Chapter Four

Doors along the corridor began to fly open, disgruntled voices emerging to echo into the hall.

"What the hell—"

"Hey, what's going on?"

Meredith jerked her head up. *Oh God.* She had to get it together. She didn't just have a murder on her hands. She had a houseful of people to tend to, a group that would need her to maintain some semblance of order and control.

She'd just barely managed to get a grip on her emotions when her guests began to appear in their doorways. Almost as soon as they appeared, they slammed to a stop as soon as they laid eyes on the sight in the middle of the hall.

"Oh, my God! Haley!"

Rachel peered out from behind Scott's shoulder, both of their faces white.

Alex cleared his throat. "Is she—"

"We should probably check to be sure," Tom murmured behind her.

Before Meredith could respond, he quickly moved past her. Bending on his knee beside Haley, he pressed a hand to her neck. A few seconds later, his expression fell further, his mouth forming a grim line that told Meredith what he'd found before he glanced up at her and gave his head a small shake.

Rachel let out an anguished groan.

Jessica, whose screams had begun to die down, picked up again, her screeching growing louder and more feverish.

Pushing past Scott, Rachel walked up to Jessica and grabbed her by both shoulders, shaking her gently. "Jess, stop it! That's not helping!"

Whether it was the words or the shaking, Jessica seemed to snap out of it slightly, her screams finally fading, turning into whimpers. "But she's—"

"Yes," Rachel said, a noticeable tremor in her voice. She glanced back at Haley. "She's dead."

"Who could have done this?" a man asked—Alex, Meredith registered a moment later—his voice heavy with shock and disbelief.

"It's the killer!" Jessica shrieked. "The same one who murdered the first woman who came here to be married! The killer is still on the loose, still here!"

"No," Meredith said firmly, not about to let the rumor take hold. "The killer was caught and, more important, is dead now."

Jessica whirled on her, her face twisting with hatred. "Why should we believe you? Maybe you just said that to trick people into coming here again. Maybe you lied about that the way you did about Brad."

The words were like a slap to her face, and Meredith nearly recoiled. As soon as she had the impulse, she knew it was exactly what she couldn't do. She couldn't afford to show the slightest weakness to any of these people—not now. And damned if she'd let this woman have the satisfaction of knowing she'd hurt her—not ever.

Shaking inside, Meredith summoned every bit of strength she had and kept the reaction off her face. She held the woman's gaze, staring her down.

"You don't have to believe me," she said, her voice even

and steady. "I'm telling the truth. What you choose to believe is up to you. But if you don't have anything helpful to contribute, please keep quiet while the rest of us work through this."

Jessica actually did recoil at the statement. Out of the corner of her eye Meredith saw a few eyebrows go up on the several of the others' faces, too. *Good,* she thought. Better they all know right now that she wasn't messing around. Not only would it be easier for her to keep things under control, it would make them all calmer knowing someone was.

"Besides, Jess," Greg said with a wobbly grin. "That killer went after brides, not maids of honor. Right, Meredith?"

"Shut up, Greg," Scott said darkly. "You're not helping."

"Why not?" Greg asked. "That should make her feel better."

"Jess," Tom interjected. "Did you see anyone or anything in the hall when you found Haley?"

Jessica appeared to consider the question. "I—I don't think so. But I really wasn't paying attention. I came out into the hall, and that's when I saw her. I didn't really notice anything else."

"What were you even doing in the hall in the middle of the night?" Alex asked.

"I had to use the bathroom," she said with a touch of defensiveness. It was a believable explanation. Sutton Hall had been built in the 1870s and only the larger suites, both in the towers and right next to them, had en suite bathrooms. Scott and Rachel's room had one, but the rest of the wedding party were using the two bathrooms along the hall.

"What do you want to do?" Tom asked, directing the question to Meredith. He'd risen to his feet and stood facing her. The sound of the calmness in his voice soothed her nerves just as much as she hoped hers did for the others. She nearly smiled at him in gratitude.

Meredith thought quickly. "First we need to call the police. I don't suppose anyone's cell is working?"

Several of the group shook their heads. Tom dug into his pocket and pulled out his phone. After a moment of staring at the screen, he shook his head. "Mine still isn't."

"I tried the landline a little while ago to test it and it was still working. Hopefully it still is."

"Even if you reach them, will they be able to get through in this weather?" Scott asked.

Meredith hesitated the slightest moment before admitting, "Maybe not." She saw the panic flash across several faces and quickly added, "But I don't know that for sure. Let me call and see what they say first. This is my first time up here in a storm this bad. The locals might be better at getting around in this kind of snow." She wasn't holding out much hope, but for the time being, it was better if everyone had at least a little. "Why doesn't everyone come down and wait in the living room while I make the call?"

"What about Haley?" Rachel asked quietly. Meredith saw she was still staring at her fallen friend. "We can't just leave her lying there."

Meredith glanced down at the body. Haley's eyes were now closed. Tom must have done it, a gesture of respect Meredith appreciated. "At the moment, this is a crime scene. We shouldn't move anything until I speak with the police and see when they might be able to get here and how they'd like us to proceed. Let's all go downstairs and I'll make that call."

She turned and started for the stairs, hoping the others would follow. A few moments later, she heard their muffled footsteps on the carpet behind her and exhaled slightly in relief.

The chandelier was aglow in the main foyer, shining sparkling rays of light across the staircase and marble floor below. Still, as Meredith reached the top of the stairs and peered down, she had to suppress a shudder. With no lights coming from the front windows or side halls, the foyer still seemed dim somehow, heavy with darkness and shadows. Meredith had never noticed before how the beams from the chandelier were diamond-shaped, pointed like little knives. There were small spaces between them, spaces that seemed darker, and there were so many places along the edge of the room they didn't reach, leaving them in shadow.

She didn't let herself hesitate, plunging down the stairs without missing a step. She kept her spine straight and her stride even, tamping down on the butterflies in her stomach. She couldn't let anyone know she was the slightest bit on edge. They moved in silence down the grand staircase, the rugs silencing the sound of their steps, emphasizing the eeriness of their progression. Only when her feet hit the bottom and they veered off the rugs onto the marble floor did they make a sound, echoing into the high ceilings above.

The living room was just off the main hall. Meredith reached for the doors, ignoring the nervous tremor that quaked through her, and pushed them open. Flipping the switch inside the door, she flooded the room with light. A quick glance around the room revealed that everything appeared as it should.

She stepped aside to let them enter. "Here we are."

The living room was the former front parlor, a big, comfortable space made for people to gather together and socialize. When she and Adam had taken over Sutton Hall, one of her first missions had been to renovate this room, figuring it would be the place most of their guests would want to come together to relax and hang out. The sofas and tables were set in a variety of arrangements, some to accommodate big groups, some for private conversations. It was a room they were all familiar with, having gathered there after dinner, where she and Ellen had served them drinks. It was one reason she'd suggested the room, figuring they'd be more comfortable here than anywhere else, since it wasn't a strange place.

But as the group began to filter in Meredith didn't miss the way they glanced around the space uneasily, as though expecting someone to jump out at them at any moment. No one took a seat, all of them moving to the center and standing there restlessly.

Greg immediately zeroed in on the bar on one wall and headed straight for it.

"Don't you think you had enough at dinner?" Scott asked.

"Clearly not, because I am way too sober for this," Greg called back over his shoulder. "Anyone else want anything?"

"What the hell," Alex muttered. "I can't think of a better time for a drink. Scotch neat."

"Coming right up," Greg said.

Jessica wrapped her arms around herself. "Where's the phone?"

"The closest one is in the study," Meredith said. "I'll be right back."

"I'll come with you," Tom said. He'd stopped in the entryway beside her. She shot him a look in surprise. He stared back, his expression serious. "You probably shouldn't be wandering around alone. At least not until we have a better idea what we're dealing with."

Her first instinct was to glance at the others. At the last second she managed to hold the impulse in check.

Wasn't the killer someone in this room? It was what Meredith had assumed. Despite what Jessica had said, the killer was most likely someone who'd come here with Haley, someone who knew her.

That might be a dangerous assumption to make, but now that he'd raised the prospect, the idea of walking through the house alone didn't hold much appeal.

Meredith nodded. "All right. Let's make that call."

THE STUDY WAS on the ground floor in the front tower of the west wing. Adam had converted it into his office when they'd taken over Sutton Hall. Meredith quickly made her way there, keeping an eye out around her at all times, fully aware of Tom following close behind.

As she stepped into the room, her gaze immediately went to the phone sitting on the desk at the other side. Mouthing a silent prayer, she crossed to the phone, picked up the receiver and raised it to her ear.

And heard nothing.

It took a second for the echoing silence to sink in. She waited, still expecting the sound of a dial tone to kick in, to hear something, anything.

Then reality hit her like a blow to the chest, panic rushing through her veins. "No, no, no..." With growing desperation she pressed on the switch hook several times, hoping the dial tone would finally kick in, praying there was only some kind of delay. She glanced at the base and where the cord disappeared into the wall, confirming everything was connected as it should be.

The receiver remained utterly, terrifyingly silent.

Dead.

When there was no way to deny it any longer, she slowly lowered the receiver and stood there, trying to process the situation. Behind her the windows shook under the force of the howling wind. The sound seemed to echo in the emptiness of the room, until she was surrounded by it on all sides.

"Nothing?" Tom asked softly.

He must have stopped in the doorway. His voice sounded

very far away, making her feel more isolated. Like she was. Like they all were.

Meredith shook her head. "There must be a line down somewhere."

"Do you have anything else? Maybe a radio of some kind?"

"No," she had to admit. "The previous owner was pretty much a recluse, and probably never saw the need of trying to get in touch with the outside world if the phones went out. We talked about getting a satellite phone just in case we ever needed one, but never got around to it. We didn't have any blizzards like this last winter and never lost phone service. And it's only October. None of us expected a storm this bad so early...."

"We barely made it up the mountain to begin with, and that was seven hours ago," Tom observed. "The storm's gotten a lot worse since then. I can't imagine there's any way we'll be able to get out."

Meredith would have given anything to say he was wrong, but she couldn't. "No," she agreed. "We have a plow that can be attached to the front of a truck, but it can't possibly be safe to use in these whiteout conditions. That's even if we could get to the garage through the snow. And even though the weather never got this bad last winter, there were still a few times it took us a day to dig out. I have to think it'll take at least a couple days to dig out from this—and that's after the storm ends."

They fell silent, the implications terrifying—and impossible to ignore.

"So we're on our own then," Tom said gently.

She nodded shortly, trying to fight the panic rising in her throat. "Yes." On their own. Trapped. For days.

With a killer among them.

Chapter Five

Tom watched the emotions wash over Meredith's face. Dismay. Fear. Resignation. He'd seen them lurking beneath the surface as she'd dealt with the situation upstairs, but she'd done an admirable job hiding them as much as possible, keeping a cool, calm facade. That was gone now, her feelings bare and plain to see. She looked lost, as though the world had just come crashing down on her and she had no idea what to do next.

It wouldn't have been a good look for anybody but somehow seemed especially wrong on this woman's face. His gut clenched at the sight. He automatically stepped forward and started toward her, the need to do something, say something, to make it better rising from the pit of his stomach.

Before he could, she abruptly lifted her head and spun away toward the door. "I have to get to Ellen and Rick," she said, her voice wobbly. "Make sure they…know what's happening."

He had a feeling *make sure they're all right* was what she'd started to say. "Okay," he agreed. "Let's go."

She was already brushing by him as he said it, her strides long and full of purpose. He quickly moved to follow as she pulled the door open and plunged back out into the hallway.

She headed toward the back of the house, away from

the front hall and living room where they'd left the others, down another long corridor.

She plowed forward, her head bowed slightly, her movements rushed and uneven. Concern rippled through him. "Hey."

When she didn't react to the word, he caught her elbow to stop her progress. A split second after his hand made contact, he felt the tremor rip through her body, every inch of her tensing even more than she already was. A strong reaction, far stronger than normal for such a minor touch. He suspected he knew the reason for it, unease roiling in his gut.

Still, she did stop. He dropped his hand. "Are you okay?"

She nodded tersely, her head bent. "I'm fine. You just startled me."

It had been more than that. He didn't doubt it for a second. Her reaction had been too fierce, too defensive. "Maybe you could stand to take a breath. Everything's been happening so fast. You haven't really had a chance to process any of this."

She mustered a smile without meeting his eyes. "And I don't have time to now. I appreciate the thought though."

She stood there, her head down, her body still tight with tension, as if it was still protecting itself. The sight drove a hard lump to his throat, and suddenly he had to know. It really wasn't any of his business, but he couldn't hold back the question.

"About what Jess said…" he said softly. "You didn't lie about what happened with Brad, did you?"

She winced, her expression saying she would give anything not to answer the question. He was about to withdraw it when she finally gave her head a tight shake, still not meeting his eyes. "No. I didn't."

Anger surged from the pit of his stomach in a rush, for

what had been done to her, toward the bastard she'd been married to whose face Tom couldn't even remember. He struggled to keep the emotion off his expression and out of his voice. "I'm sorry," he said gently, the words pathetically inadequate. He actually felt stupid saying them. "For Jess. For…everything."

"Thanks," she said flatly. "But that's pretty much the least of my concerns now."

"Understood. You're sure you're okay?"

"I think I have to be, don't I?" She glanced up at him, realization dawning on her features. "What about you? She was your friend."

Tom nodded, a combination of guilt and sorrow building in his chest at the reminder. He knew Haley was dead— murdered. He'd seen it with his own eyes, felt her cool skin with his own fingers. But it didn't seem real. None of this seemed like it could actually be happening.

"I actually hadn't spoken to her at all since college, at least not until today. I should have stayed in touch with her." Heck, he should have done a better job of keeping in touch with all of them. Even Scott, the one he'd spoken to the most, was someone he'd only been in contact with a couple times a year, if that. If there was one thing this weekend had already proved, it was what a lousy job he'd done maintaining the friendships that had once been the cornerstone of his world.

"I only got a chance to catch up with her a little at the airport. And now she's gone." He could barely wrap his head around it. It was hard to believe that the same woman who'd been laughing and talking with them just a few hours ago was now lying dead in the upstairs hallway, gone forever.

Meredith reached out, hesitating slightly before placing her hand on his arm. "I'm sorry," she said, genuine sympathy shining in her deep brown eyes.

"Thanks."

With a tight nod, she pulled her hand away, its absence inexplicably making him feel colder. "Come on," she said, sending an uneasy glance down the corridor. "We should keep moving."

Tom followed her gaze. The hallway was empty and well-lit. He didn't spot a single shadow. So why did it suddenly appear so impossibly long and dim somehow, every doorway seeming to contain a possible threat?

As if sensing the same thing he did, she shuddered lightly.

"You're right," he agreed. "Let's go."

She quickly took off again, regaining her earlier speed. Tom fell into step beside her. He knew she had to be concerned about her employees. But as he thought about the people they were seeking out, he realized there was a very good chance that one of them was responsible for what had happened upstairs.

He pictured them—the big, muscular handyman with the friendly grin who'd helped them with their bags and the full-figured, pleasant-faced cook who'd served dinner. He couldn't immediately see either of them committing the gruesome act upstairs. But who else was here?

"How much do you know about your employees?" Tom asked carefully.

"Everything possible. After what happened here before, Adam—that's my brother—conducted practically government-level background checks on them to make sure there were no skeletons in their closets or issues we needed to know about. After what happened before we weren't taking any chances."

"Still, there could be something that wouldn't show up in a background check, some secret reason to lead one of them to do this."

"I trust them absolutely," she said firmly.

It was on the tip of his tongue to ask if she'd felt the same way about the previous staff. He bit back the question, figuring he'd pushed her enough tonight.

"It looked like a kitchen knife was what was used," he pointed out. "As far as I know, no one from the wedding party got close to the kitchen."

"I didn't see it that closely. And Ellen had a few knives out for the roast and the rest of dinner, didn't she?"

Thinking back, he realized she was right. "Did you notice any of them missing after dinner?"

"No," she admitted. "But I wasn't keeping track of them. She shot him a glance. "What about you? You haven't seen most of your friends in years. They could have changed. They could have motives you know nothing about."

Tom couldn't exactly argue with her. He suspected many of them had changed. But the idea that one of them could have changed enough to become a killer—and kill one of their own friends—was inconceivable.

Before he could answer, they arrived at a back hallway on the first floor not far from the kitchen. Probably a logical place for the household staff to be staying.

Meredith walked up to one of the doors. Raising her hand, she hesitated for a brief moment before knocking. "Ellen? It's Meredith."

There was no immediate response, likely not a surprise considering what time it was. The woman was probably asleep. *Unless she's been up to something else,* he thought.

A darker thought drifted through his mind, inspiring a hint of guilt. *Unless something happened to this woman, as well*.

They waited a few moments. Tom didn't detect any sounds from within the room. His unease growing, he shot a glance down the hallway in both directions. "Is Rick staying down here, too? I can get him."

Meredith nodded. "Yes, he's—"

The door of the cook's room suddenly opened slightly, drawing their attention back to it. Seconds later, Ellen appeared in the gap. Still holding the door partway shut, she peered at them, eyes wide with concern. "What is it? What's wrong?"

"Something's happened," Meredith said. She took a deep breath before continuing, and he could sense how difficult it was for her to say the rest. "There's been a murder. One of the guests has been killed."

At first the other woman simply blinked at her with a complete lack of comprehension. "Who— When—" She swallowed. "Who did it?"

"We don't know," Meredith admitted. "Can you come with us? I think it would be safer if everyone stuck together."

For a moment, doubt flickered across the woman's face, and Tom had a feeling she wanted to say no. She was probably thinking she'd be safer staying where she was. He couldn't fault her for the idea.

He studied the cook's face, trying to get a better read on her. He hadn't gotten much of an impression of the woman that evening. Truth be told, while they were being served dinner, he'd been too busy watching Meredith to pay much attention to the other woman. She'd simply been a smiling presence working beside Meredith.

She wasn't smiling now, of course. She looked appropriately shocked and scared. He just didn't know her well enough to know whether the reaction was genuine.

"Of course," Ellen said. "Just let me get dressed."

"Go ahead," Meredith said. "Let me wake Rick. He needs to know what's happening, too."

"What's going on?"

The voice came out of nowhere. Tom quickly jerked his head to the side to spot the man a few yards away, standing in the open door of another room farther down the hall. It was Rick.

Tom nearly swore. The man had managed to come out into the hall without any of them noticing. Tom was going to have to do a better job staying on guard and aware of his surroundings.

"Rick," Meredith said. "We were just coming to get you." She quickly explained the situation as she had to Ellen. "Will you come with us to the main living room?"

"Sure," he said, without hesitating as Ellen had.

He didn't seem at all disturbed by the idea that there was a killer in Sutton Hall. Or maybe he figured he could take care of himself. From the look of him, Tom wasn't sure he could disagree. A big man in his thirties, Rick was tall and clearly muscled even beneath the baggy sweatshirt and shorts he wore. When he'd helped them with the bags, he'd been friendly and all smiles. There was no trace of that now, his expression serious and attentive. Something in his steady, watchful gaze made Tom think of a soldier or a police officer. He wondered again what the man's background was.

Ellen's door opened, and the woman stepped out, now wearing a robe over her nightclothes.

"All right," she said solemnly, looking at the three of them. "I'm ready."

With a nod, Meredith turned to lead the way. Ellen followed her. Tom motioned for Rick to precede him. From the way the man eyed him, Rick wasn't sure he wanted to. Maybe he figured it made sense for him to bring up the rear, since he worked here.

After a moment, Rick moved to follow Ellen. The tightness in his chest easing slightly, Tom fell into line behind him, casting one last glance back.

Maybe he was being overly cautious, but Tom wasn't ready to put his back to the other man. Or to the cook, for that matter.

Meredith might trust them but, for the time being, he couldn't afford to.

THE LIVING ROOM doors were shut when they made it back to the front foyer. Tom wasn't surprised. Given what was happening, he couldn't blame the others for wanting to feel a little more secure.

Instead of heading toward the living room, Meredith crossed the foyer to the front door. Unlocking it, she pulled it open.

The wind immediately burst in, lashing at them. Standing a few feet behind her, Tom saw his earlier conclusion had been right. In fact, seeing it for himself suddenly made it seem so much worse. The snow came up to the middle of her thighs, and that was just by the door. It seemed to get higher the farther out he looked. The vehicles they'd driven up the mountain had been left in front of the building, but there was no sign of them in the snow. And more flurries continued to flood down from the sky, the air nearly as white as the piles already on the ground.

Meredith pushed the door shut, filling the hall with silence once more.

"Not getting out of here anytime soon," Rick observed.

"No," Meredith agreed softly. "Let's get back to the others."

She quickly moved to the living room, the rest of them following close behind. Reaching the door, she hesitated briefly, then knocked before opening it. Warning them someone was coming in so they weren't surprised and scared by someone yanking the door open, Tom figured, impressed by her consideration.

Everyone in the room looked up as they entered. As the last one in, Tom pulled the door shut behind him.

"Did you reach the police?" Rachel asked, a touch of hope in her voice.

Meredith took a breath. "No," she said calmly. There was no hint on her face or in her voice of the devastation he knew she'd felt after the call. "The phone is out. It looks like we have no way to reach anyone."

A chorus of dismayed sounds rose from the group. "Then what are we going to do?" Scott asked. "Is there any way we can get out of here?"

"Unfortunately, no," Meredith said again. "There's already too much snow on the ground and it's still coming down too hard. We do have a plow capable of being connected to one of our pickup trucks that can be used to clear the snow, but the way it's coming down out there, we can't even get to the garage to reach the plow."

"Not to mention it won't do much good with the snow still coming down the way it is," Rick noted.

"So how long will it be until we can get out of here?" Jessica demanded.

Meredith hesitated briefly before admitting, "At least a few days."

"A few days?" Jessica screeched. "So what are we supposed to do, just sit here while there's a killer running loose?"

"If we all stay calm and look out for each other, we should be safe until the storm ends," Tom said.

Jessica's expression made it clear what she thought about that.

"Are there any weapons in the house?" Scott asked.

Meredith slowly shook her head. "There used to be an

antique gun collection, but we sold it." She swallowed. "It seemed unsafe to have in the house with guests."

A subdued silence fell over the room. Tom studied the others' faces as they processed the news that they were trapped here. He knew they all had to have been hoping for a different answer, no matter how unrealistic that was. Now that last bit of hope had been snuffed out. There was no denying it. They were thoroughly trapped for the time being.

Still, as he observed their expressions, Tom had to wonder if everyone was upset about the news. How did the killer feel knowing that they weren't going anywhere? Upset that there was no possibility of escape for himself, too…or pleased that the rest of them would still be here, still available to be attacked next?

He looked for the slightest hint that anyone was anything but discouraged at the news, but he didn't detect anyone's reaction being out of the ordinary.

Then he realized what he was doing. Shock jolted through him at the knowledge. Was he really considering the possibility that one of these people he'd known for years, people he'd once considered his closest friends, was not just a killer, but some kind of psychopath wanting to strike again? If anything he should be looking at the ones he didn't know, Rick and Ellen, considering them more likely candidates.

But as he surveyed the assembled group, he knew that was exactly what he'd been doing, and what he probably had to do. One of these people likely had a better motive to kill Haley than a complete stranger would. And for the sake of the rest of them, he had to consider that one of them might be a threat to the others.

"I'm still having a hard time understanding who could have done this," Scott murmured.

"Can any of you think of any reason why someone would

have wanted to hurt Haley?" Meredith asked. "Did anyone have any known problems with her?"

Everyone looked at one another, as though expecting someone else to have the answer. No one responded.

"No," Rachel said finally. "She was one of the nicest people you could ever hope to meet. She's the last person I could ever imagine anyone wanting to hurt." Her voice trembled on the final words, and Scott reached out and wrapped an arm around her. She leaned into him, turning her face into his chest.

"Are you sure there isn't anyone else in the house?" Alex asked.

Meredith shook her head. "No, this is everyone."

"But are you *sure* of that," Alex pressed in what Tom imagined was his hardnosed reporter voice. "This is a massive place. There's no way there could be someone else here that you don't know about?"

Meredith hesitated, seeming to consider the idea. At the sight of that pause, Tom could practically feel the tension in the room go up another notch.

"We're so isolated that anyone would have needed a car to get up here, and I haven't seen any unexpected vehicles around. Have you, Rick?"

The man shook his head. "No."

"Have you had any trucks making deliveries for the wedding?" Alex asked. "Is there a chance someone could have come with someone else and simply not left?"

Meredith paused again, but this time was quicker to answer. "It's possible, but very unlikely. For one thing, someone would have had to get into the house without Ellen, Rick or I noticing. I honestly don't believe there's anyone else here."

Tom fought a frown. Given the size of Sutton Hall, there could be any number of places someone could have sneaked in unnoticed. He kept his mouth shut, not about to bring that up now. The group was tense enough as it is. And she was right, it did seem unlikely. Still, it was something they might have to consider.

"Then who could have done this?" Rachel said.

Tom watched several heads turn toward Rick and Ellen, viewing them with suspicion. Rick and Ellen looked back at the group with equal distrust.

"Maybe it was *her,*" Jessica said sullenly, looking straight at Meredith. She leaned back in her seat, her arms folded over her chest, her eyes narrowed to slits.

"It couldn't have been Meredith," Tom said, barely managing to keep a hold of his temper. "She was with me."

Tom sensed the others' attention shift to him and Meredith. Jessica's eyes widened, her brows shooting sky-high as she glanced from him to Meredith and back again. "I didn't realize the two of you were so *close.*"

"We're not," Tom said, though as soon as the words were out they felt wrong somehow. "We were in the kitchen. I went down for a snack. We both came when we heard you screaming. And she was right earlier. If you don't have anything helpful to contribute, you might as well be quiet and let the rest of us work this out."

"This isn't your damn TV show, Tom," Jessica sniped. "We're not part of some *production* for you to *manage,* Mr. Producer. You're not in charge here."

"No, *I* am," Meredith said. Tom thought he heard a tremor in her voice, so light he wasn't sure he hadn't imagined it. She glanced around the room at the others, her gaze steady. "Unless anyone has a problem with that?"

No one voiced an objection. Jess's eyes narrowed, her face going red, but she held her tongue, pressing her lips together tightly.

"Good," Meredith said. Tom could practically sense her

relief. "Now I think we should all try to get some sleep. It's been a long day, and sitting here throwing around a bunch of accusations isn't accomplishing anything. Hopefully after we get some rest, we'll all be thinking clearer and we can figure out what to do next."

"An excellent idea!" Greg proclaimed, raising his glass in acknowledgment. Tom noted that his hand shook as he made the gesture. "I could use some shut-eye myself."

"I'm not sure how much sleep I'll be able to get," Rachel said quietly. A few others murmured in agreement.

"That's why it helps to have a drink," Greg said.

Rachel shot him a look, her nose wrinkling in distaste. "I don't think it would help at all if the rest of us started drinking as much as you."

"Oh, you'd be surprised. It's very good at helping you forget things. For a little while at least…" he added almost as an afterthought, his voice trailing off, his tone surprisingly subdued.

"There's just one thing we have to deal with," Tom said. He almost hated to raise the subject, but there was no way around it. "Haley."

The reminder that Haley was still up there, lying in the middle of the hall, plunged the group back into a grim, uncomfortable silence.

"It's still a crime scene," Alex pointed out. "The police probably wouldn't want us to move her."

Rachel looked at him in horror. "So what do you want to do, Alex? Leave her lying there in the middle of the hall for *days?*"

Alex lifted his hands defensively. "I'm not saying it's what I want to do! I'm just saying it's normal procedure."

"We are *not* leaving her there!" Rachel insisted.

Tom had to agree with her. There was no way of knowing when they'd be able to reach anyone. Even if they did, it would be at least three or four days until the police could arrive. There was no way they could simply leave the body in the middle of the hall that long. It would be utterly inhumane to someone most of the people in this room considered a friend. And everyone's nerves were already frayed, he didn't want to think how tense things would be after a few days of living with Haley's body there in their midst.

"You're right," Meredith said calmly. "We can't leave her there. It may be normal procedure, but these are not normal circumstances. We can move her to a room at the end of the hall until the police get here. If the police have a problem with it, they can charge me with whatever they want. I'll worry about it later. But we should probably try to document the scene first so they can see what it looked like. Even if it's not admissible as evidence, at least they'll be able to see it."

"I can do it," Tom suggested. "I brought a couple cameras for the wedding, both a video and a Nikon." A few of the others had actually kidded him about it on the drive up when Scott had mentioned it, pointing out that everyone's cell phone had a camera on it these days. He'd thought they deserved better images than those captured by a camera phone. That seemed even more vital now that they were talking about things like evidence.

"Thank you."

Jessica suddenly spoke up again. "You can hate me for saying it, but somebody has to. How do we know the two of you won't try to destroy any evidence?"

Silence fell again. Tom noted that no one spoke up to say the idea was ridiculous.

"If it would make everyone more comfortable, we could probably use at least one more person to help move…the body, if someone wants to come up?"

He glanced around the group for volunteers. In spite

of being the one who'd raised the objection, Jessica didn't speak up, her lips fixed in a pout. He saw Rachel grip Scott's hand. Even if she hadn't, Tom doubted Scott would have wanted to leave her. As Tom thought it, Scott looked up and met his eyes, a hint of apology in his. It wasn't as though Greg would be much help, his head already starting to droop.

"Why don't you go, Alex?" Jessica said. "Or would it be too hard for you to see her like that?"

There seemed to be a challenge in the question, one Alex didn't miss as he glared back at her.

Before he could respond, Rick stepped forward. "I'll come with you," he said. "She's right. Her friends shouldn't have to see her like that or have to help move her."

"Thanks, Rick." Meredith glanced around the room, lingering slightly on Jess. "Any objections?"

Jess pressed her lips together as though she was barely managing to hold one back. She didn't say anything. Neither did anyone else.

"All right," Meredith said. "We'll return as soon as we can to let you know you can come up."

From the looks on their faces none of them was particularly eager to do so. Not that Tom blamed them, not with the memory of what had happened up there still fresh in their minds.

Tom wasn't looking forward to moving the body, but it had to be done. He hadn't been much of a friend to Haley since college, but at least he could do this for her. Not only did Haley deserve to be treated with care, but there might be clues that could indicate who'd done this to her.

And if there was no way out of here, the most important thing was to identify the killer in their midst.

Before he—or she—could strike again.

Chapter Six

The sight of the body lying in the middle of the hallway wasn't any easier to see the second time. As soon as Meredith stepped onto the second floor and spotted Haley there, she had to repress a shudder, the wave of revulsion rising in her belly.

"Let me get my cameras," Tom said softly. Moving past them, he headed toward his room, carefully avoiding the body in the center of the hall.

Beside her, she heard Rick swear under his breath, and she realized this was his first time seeing the body. She glanced over at him, his face paler than it had been moments earlier. "Thank you for doing this," she murmured. "You don't have to, though, if you don't want to. I know it's above and beyond the call of duty."

"It's okay," he said. "I can handle it. It's not my first time seeing a dead body. But I guess you never really get used to it, and I've sure never seen anything like this."

She'd forgotten for a moment that Rick had served in the army and done several tours of duty overseas. She should have realized he'd seen the dead before, though from his expression there was something uniquely horrifying about this.

Tom returned with the handheld video camera and Nikon he'd brought. Meredith and Rick waited out of the way as he slowly and methodically went about documenting the scene, first on still images, then on video.

It was fascinating watching him work. He took his time recording every inch of the body and area around it. The hands that held the camera were steady and true, his gaze just as stable as he focused on the screen on the camera. When he moved in front of her, she caught glimpses of the screen, observing how he zoomed in and out to give both a close and wider view of what he was recording.

Meredith watched him bend on one knee, focusing the camera on the floor beside the body. Curious, she leaned closer to see what he was fixing on.

Then she spotted them, the series of red marks on the carpet leading from the body. "Is that blood?"

"Looks like it," he confirmed.

Meredith followed the trail with her eyes, from where it began at the body to a door several feet away.

"That's the door to Haley's room," she noted just as he began to turn the camera on it. Why would there be a trail of blood from Haley's room toward the body? She supposed the most obvious answer was…

She stepped forward. "Do you want me to open it?" she asked, referring to the door.

Tom never took his eyes from the viewer on the camera. "I think you should."

Meredith reached out and released the door, then slowly nudged it open. The light was still on inside. Almost immediately she spotted the blood just inside the door, leading farther into the room, growing denser as it proceeded.

Tom carefully moved inside, tracking the blood with his camera. Meredith followed a few steps behind, unable to resist, even as a little tremor of unease rumbled through her. She felt Rick fall into line behind her.

Tom came to an abrupt stop, aiming the camera toward

the center of the room. Meredith peered around his shoulder, her breath hitching as she saw what he was recording. There was no mistaking the blood splattered across the center of the floor, the pool thick and wide on the blue rug she'd chosen and laid in place herself.

"*This* is the murder scene," she whispered hoarsely.

"I would bet on it," Tom said.

"So she was killed in here and then moved out into the hallway." It certainly explained why the trail of blood got smaller as it reached the door. "But why?"

"Because the killer wanted her to be discovered."

It was Rick who drew the conclusion, but Tom nodded an instant later. "It makes the most sense. If she'd simply been left in here, she most likely wouldn't have been found until morning, maybe when she didn't come down for breakfast. Putting her in the middle of the hallway, where someone would absolutely see her if they needed to use the bathroom, guaranteed she would be found sooner."

Goose bumps raised along her skin as the implications of it sank in.

"The killer wanted everyone to know this had happened," Meredith said numbly. "He—or she—wanted everyone to be afraid."

"I'd say mission accomplished then," Tom said.

"It makes sense, since the knife was left in her," Rick said. "It couldn't have been easy to move her like that. Or else the killer stuck the knife back in after she was moved."

"The killer wanted to make sure everyone not only knew that she was dead, but exactly *how* she died." It would have been horrifying enough to find Haley lying in the middle of the floor with her chest coated in blood. But actually seeing the big knife, leaving no doubt exactly what had killed her, had made it so much worse.

Meredith let out a long, deep breath, trying to control

her racing pulse. "It's not just to scare everybody, is it? It's a warning. Whoever it is intends to kill again."

As much as she wanted someone to disagree, no one argued the conclusion.

"Maybe we should get out of here," Tom said. "I have everything I need."

"Good idea," Meredith agreed. She reached in her pocket for her keys. "I'll lock the room so no one else can come in until the police get here."

They quickly filed back to the exit. Rick and Tom ducked through first. Shutting off the light, Meredith pulled the door shut and locked it behind her.

Turning around, her eyes fell back on the trail of blood on the floor. Frowning, she automatically checked the floor around the rest of the body. "There's no blood leading to any of the other rooms."

Tom nodded. "I noticed that."

"That's strange, isn't it? I'm no blood expert, but wouldn't the killer have gotten some on him—or her?" Given Haley's injuries, it seemed inevitable.

"I would say so," Rick agreed.

"Yet they managed to not leave a trail leading back to them."

"Whoever it is was very careful," Tom observed. "Most likely, the killer knew what he was doing."

Meredith didn't miss the glance Tom shot at Rick, his steady gaze full of suspicion. A wave of indignation rose inside her, and she had to bite back the retort that rose to her lips, not wanting to say anything in front of Rick. In all fairness she knew Tom had every right to suspect him. Everyone had to be considered a possible suspect, but it only made sense that he would especially question someone who was a complete stranger to him.

But Meredith was equally convinced Rick couldn't be

responsible. "There's something else," Meredith said. She forced herself to look back at the body. "That knife," she said, indicating the item still jutting out of Jessica's chest. "I don't recognize the handle. It's definitely not one from the house."

She watched Tom process that information in light of what they'd discussed earlier. "Which means it probably belongs to whoever did this. They must have brought it with them."

It did seem like the most likely explanation. The only alternative she could think of would be that the knife belonged to Haley and it had somehow been used against her, but she couldn't imagine why Haley would have brought a knife like that. No, the most reasonable explanation was that it had been brought here for this very purpose. "So this wasn't something that happened on the spur of the moment. It was premeditated. Whoever it was came here intending to do this...."

Her voice faded as it hit her just how much worse this kept getting.

The killer wasn't just careful and methodical. He—or she—was prepared. And if this was what happened on the first night, there was no telling what the killer had planned for the next few days.

She struggled to think of something, anything that might indicate who could have done this. "Do you think it's a man?" she asked numbly. "It would have taken some strength to move the body, right?" Neither Rachel or Jessica was particularly big. She couldn't see either of them having much in the way of arm strength.

Ellen, on the other hand...

Meredith tried to shut down the thought before it could form, not wanting to go there, even as a little voice deep inside whispered that she was going to have to at least consider the possibility.

All eyes went to the woman on the floor. "Not necessarily," Rick said after a moment. "She's not very big. It wouldn't have taken much to move her. All the killer would've had to do is grab her under her shoulders and drag her out here."

Meredith slowly raised her eyes to look at him, unable to resist the impulse. Out of the corner of her eye, she sensed Tom do the same.

Rick held up his hands, no doubt picking up on what they were so obviously wondering. "I'm just guessing here. I know about moving stuff. I'm saying that's how I would do it, not that I did."

"Nobody thinks you did, Rick," Meredith said automatically, shaking off her momentary doubts and doing her best not to glance at Tom. "So it could have been anyone." Even Rachel or—

Another thought occurred to her. "I didn't see any blood on Jessica, did you?" Meredith asked Tom.

Tom was silent for a moment. Whether it was because he was thinking about it or because he didn't like having to consider Jessica as a suspect, Meredith couldn't tell. "No, but there's always the possibility she quickly changed, then came back into the hall and started screaming to make it look like she'd just discovered the body."

Her screams had seemed genuine, Meredith thought, the memory of them enough to send her skin crawling again. But that didn't necessarily mean anything. "She is an actress, isn't she?"

Tom met her eyes with clear reluctance. "Yes."

"She was awful quick to start throwing accusations around," Rick said.

Meredith couldn't argue with him about that. He was

right, and he hadn't even been there when Haley's body had been found and Jessica had first started accusing people. "I don't know her well enough to know if that's suspicious or typical of her personality."

"Unfortunately, I can't say, either," Tom said. "Like Haley, I hadn't seen her in years before today. I admit she's a lot more unpleasant than I remember, but I don't know how much of that is just an indication of how much she's changed over the years."

Meredith swallowed. She should have known it wouldn't be that easy.

Tom cleared his throat. "I guess we should finish what we came here to do. The others are going to be wondering what's taking us so long."

He was right. She surveyed Haley one more time, considering how to proceed. "There's an empty room down the hall," she said finally. "We can put her in there."

"Sounds good," Tom agreed.

Retrieving a sheet from a nearby closet, Meredith spread it out on the floor. Working together, Tom and Rick placed the body on the sheet and gently wrapped it. Meredith moved ahead to open the door to the room, stepping out of the way to let them carry the body inside. They quickly did so, wasting no time stepping back out once the task was done. As soon as they were back in the hallway, Meredith locked the door.

When they were finally done with the grim task, no one seemed to be much in the mood to talk. They made their way back to the living room in silence.

Everyone gathered in the room looked up at their entrance. No one said anything, but the question was clearly in their eyes.

"It's done," Meredith confirmed. "Everyone can head up to bed."

No one gave any sign of relief, only acceptance as they began to rise from their seats.

"In the meantime," Tom said, "until we get to the bottom of this, I'd like to suggest everyone try to stay together and not go anywhere alone. It should be safer that way."

"Unless the person you're alone with is the killer," Alex said darkly.

The comment was met with a nervous silence. Meredith saw Jessica shudder. Rachel leaned a little closer into Scott.

Meredith turned to Rick and Ellen. "Would the two of you like to stay upstairs with the rest of us, so you're not so isolated on the other side of the house? There are still plenty of rooms." Even without the one that had been turned into a makeshift morgue.

Rick and Ellen glanced at each other, seeming to share a look, before turning back to Meredith. "If you don't mind, I think I'd rather stay where I am," Ellen told her.

"Me, too," Rick agreed.

"All right," Meredith said. While she wouldn't have minded having them close so she'd have a better idea whether they were safe, she could certainly understand why they would want to be away from the wedding guests. After listening to all the bickering and suspicions, being isolated on the other side of the house away from these people—one of whom might be a killer—didn't sound like a bad thing. Not to mention, Rick likely wasn't in any hurry to spend the night upstairs near the body after what he'd just had to do. "I guess I'll see you both in the morning then?"

They both nodded.

She watched them go, disappearing into the other wing and the darkness that led to the rear of the house.

The rest of the group made their way up the staircase without speaking. Meredith didn't know if it was exhaustion or the traumatic events of the past few hours that kept them quiet and subdued. She wouldn't have blamed them for either.

When they made it to the second floor, Jessica hurried to her room, quickly slamming the door shut. The sound of the lock fastening was audible down the hall.

Scott glanced back when he and Rachel reached their room, Rachel ducking inside first. "Good night," he said.

"'Night, man," Tom said. "See you tomorrow."

With a nod, Scott went inside.

Down the hall, Alex and Greg retreated to their respective rooms.

Until she and Tom were the only ones left.

Meredith felt a sudden awkwardness as they stood there in the echoing stillness of the corridor. It seemed strange. After everything they'd been through in the past few hours, she should feel comfortable around him. But there it was nonetheless.

"Thank you for your help tonight," she said. "I honestly don't know what I would have done without it."

"I'm glad I was able to do something," he said. "You're sure you're all right?"

She remembered when he'd asked her that in the downstairs hall, remembered the way his low, deep voice had washed over, remembered the kindness and concern in his eyes, much as it was now.

Remembered how she'd freaked out a little when he'd touched her, her whole body practically having a seizure at the contact.

Embarrassment flooded her at the memory, as well as fresh anger at Brad and what he'd put her through. When would that nightmare no longer have that kind of effect on her? When would she finally, fully, be able to move past what he'd done to her?

"I'm as fine as I can be," she assured him. "We should try to get some sleep. I'll see you in the morning."

"Good night."

Ducking her head, she turned away. Her room was farther down the hall away from the others. Close to where they'd put Haley, she acknowledged with a shudder. At the time she'd thought it would be best if she stayed nearby in case anyone needed anything. She'd never imagined how necessary that would prove to be.

She quickly made her way there, eyeing the closed doors she passed along the way. Prickles of warning rose along her skin, as though her instincts were telling her that any moment one of those doors could burst open and someone would lunge out at her, knife in hand....

She finally arrived at her room. Unlocking the door, she pushed it open, then glanced back.

Tom stood in his doorway, watching her.

When he saw her looking back at him, he raised his hand in acknowledgment. He made no move to enter his room, simply standing there facing her. She realized he was waiting for her to go in first, waiting to make sure she was safe and secure behind closed doors.

She knew she shouldn't read too much into it. It was exactly as he'd said earlier—they should stick together, stay in pairs. He wasn't doing for her what he wouldn't do for anyone else. It wasn't really personal.

And yet, it felt personal all the same. A heady warmth poured through her at the knowledge, at the feeling of his eyes on her. After everything that had happened and working so hard to take care of everyone else, she had to admit it felt good knowing someone was looking out for her. And to have it be this man, of all people, only made it sweeter.

With one last little wave good-night, she stepped inside and closed the door, firmly locking it behind her.

ONE DOWN...

Everything had gone even better than anticipated. It had been so easy. Haley hadn't understood how much trouble she'd been in until the very end. Then she had. She'd been terrified.

And then she was dead.

The best part had been watching the reactions of the others afterward, particularly the ones who needed to suffer. The fear in their eyes. The panic about what was happening. The realization that they were trapped. The concern that they could be next.

They were scared.

They should be.

Chapter Seven

After a few restless hours that left her feeling like she hadn't gotten any sleep at all, Meredith was awake by 6:00 a.m. Rising from the bed, she automatically moved to the window and peered out.

Nothing but a wall of white. She couldn't even see where the snow on the ground began. It was as though everything outside Sutton Hall had simply been erased. The world had been reduced to what lay inside the mansion's walls.

Trying to shake off the chill that came over her, Meredith quickly dressed. She was about to leave the room, her hand reaching for the lock she'd bolted only hours ago, when she stopped. The lock was a vivid reminder of what had happened last night, what she'd been trying to keep out.

What could be lurking on the other side of the door.

She quickly turned and scanned her surroundings, searching for something she could use as a weapon. Maybe she was being overly cautious, but she didn't think that was possible given the circumstances.

Her gaze finally fell on an empty flower vase sitting on the table by the window. Crossing to it, she picked it up, gripping it upside down by the neck. It had some weight to it, and if she hit someone with it, it would either hurt or smash against them. Either sounded good. At the very least she could throw it if necessary. It wasn't perfect, but at least it was something.

The hallway was empty when she finally stepped out of her room. She eyed the closed doors of her guests warily as she passed by. She hadn't heard anything in the night, and she hoped that meant nothing else had happened. With any luck, everyone was safely in bed, sound asleep.

Quickly making her way downstairs to the office, she checked the phone line. Silence greeted her. It was still dead.

Grimacing, she hung up the phone and headed for the kitchen. She had no idea what time everyone else would be up and expecting breakfast, but at the moment, she could certainly use some coffee.

She wondered if Ellen was awake and working on breakfast. When Meredith had hired her, they'd agreed she would be in the kitchen by six to get started on the meal, but given everything that had happened last night, Meredith wasn't sure she could count on that or if she even had any reason to.

But when she reached the door, she heard sounds of motion inside the room. She started to push through the door, only to realize at the last second that it might not be Ellen. Pausing, she slowly eased the door open and peered inside.

She exhaled when she spotted Ellen working at the counter, preparing a tray of muffins for the oven.

As soon as Meredith stepped into the room, Ellen jerked her head up. Meredith didn't miss the way the woman tensed as she looked to see who it was. Or how she relaxed slightly when she saw it was Meredith.

"Good morning," Meredith said, working up a smile.

"Morning," Ellen replied with a nod. "I wasn't sure what time everyone would be up after…everything that happened last night, but I figured I might as well get a start on things."

"Thank you," Meredith said. Moving to the island, she set her vase on the countertop. "I know this isn't what you signed on for. I wouldn't blame you if you wanted to quit on the spot and barricade yourself in your room until the police get here."

"Sounds like it'll be a while until that happens, and I've found it's best to keep busy as much as possible. Better than sitting around thinking about a killer running around, or trying to find a new job."

Meredith couldn't help but frown at the woman's words. A second later, Ellen looked up and met Meredith's eyes, a hint of apology in hers.

"I don't mean to be insensitive, but I have to be realistic, right? There's not much chance there will be any more weddings here after this."

Meredith's heart sank, a rock-hard feeling settling low in her gut. In the middle of all the madness last night, she hadn't really had time to think about it. Or maybe she just hadn't wanted to. Hearing Ellen say the words made it impossible to ignore the issue any longer.

The other woman was right, of course. There was likely no chance the wedding business could continue after this. Even if anyone actually would want to hold their wedding here, Meredith doubted she had it in her to try again. Not to mention she would always wonder if someone else would try to take advantage of Sutton Hall's history to hurt somebody. She couldn't put anyone at risk again.

A wave of sadness crashed over her. The wedding business was supposed to be her fresh start. When she'd first come here and started making plans, she'd been happier than she'd felt in a long time. She remembered the excitement of those months when she'd first begun preparing the place for guests, all the dreams she'd had of joyous celebrations, of happy couples, happy endings... She'd never imagined how horribly wrong everything would go.

An instant later, she shook off the feeling. A woman had

died. That was far worse than her dreams being dashed. She would simply have to move on and start over.

She'd done it before.

If Ellen was at all disappointed by this turn of events, she certainly didn't show it. "I have to admit, you don't sound too upset at the idea," Meredith observed.

The cook gave a little shrug and turned back to the muffins. "Something else I've learned over the years—no point being sad over things you can't control. And I have to say, maybe it is for the best."

"What do you mean?"

"To have something like this happen at another wedding…maybe there just aren't supposed to be weddings here. Sure seems that way."

Meredith frowned. "Did you feel that way before?"

Ellen hesitated for a moment before admitting, "I thought about it. Most folks around here did. Can't really blame us, can you?"

"Then why did you want to work here?"

"A job's a job. And who could have thought something this terrible would happen again?"

Indeed. The woman's attitude made sense, but Meredith couldn't help but be a little bothered by it. Then again, Ellen had no reason to be as invested in this place as much as Meredith. It really was just a job to her, not her dream.

She heard the door behind her suddenly swing open. Her pulse leaping, Meredith jerked toward the sound.

Tom stood just inside the room, holding the swinging door open. Those deep blue eyes zeroed in on her. Something that looked an awful lot like relief flashed across his face.

"There you are," he said.

At the confirmation that he'd been looking for her, her heart did a foolish, ridiculous little lurch in her chest. "Did you need something?" she asked. The words had barely left her mouth when a terrible suspicion hit her. "Did something happen?"

"No," he said quickly, stepping forward into the room. "I went by your room and there was no answer. I just wanted to make sure you were okay. Like I said last night, I'm not sure how safe it is to be wandering around here alone."

As much as she believed she didn't need his concern, she couldn't help but feel a little touched by it. "I'm fine," she assured him with a smile. "I'm surprised you're up this early. I figured everybody might want to stay in bed later after last night."

"I couldn't sleep," he admitted.

"Do you need coffee as badly as I do?" she asked.

"I'd love some."

"Coming right up." She turned toward the other woman. "Ellen, is—"

"Freshly brewed and ready to be poured." The cook nodded toward the counter.

"Thank you," Meredith said, her earlier annoyance with the woman momentarily forgotten.

"Sure thing." Her mouth curving at the corners, the cook shot her a look Meredith couldn't quite read. Then Ellen's gaze shifted to Tom for a second, her smile deepening, before she turned back to her work.

Meredith could feel a flush climbing in her cheeks. She focused on pulling two mugs from the cabinet and pouring the coffee. "I was thinking it might be worthwhile to go through Haley's things. There might be a clue or something that could indicate who might have killed her. I know it's a crime scene, but the most important thing right now is to figure out who did this. I can't sit around and do nothing knowing there's a killer on the loose."

"It's not a bad idea," he agreed, though she detected a

hint of hesitancy in his voice. She knew how hard it had to be for him to believe that one of his friends could be a killer. Maybe he was wondering if he truly wanted to find anything in Haley's room, something that could very well prove one of those friends was involved. Of course, if they didn't find anything it might be further proof that the killer wasn't one of his friends, but someone else....

Meredith resisted the instinctive urge to glance at Ellen. She wanted to believe neither of her employees was responsible. It made more sense that Haley had been killed by someone who'd known her, not a complete stranger. But if the killer wasn't a member of the wedding party, it had to be one of the staff. Rick or Ellen.

Ellen, who evidently hadn't believed the weddings should continue, and didn't seem all that upset that they wouldn't or that she'd have to find another job...

Pushing the thoughts aside, Meredith turned back to Tom and held out the coffee cup to him. "It might be good if you could document the room, as well," she said. "So the police know where everything was before we moved any of it."

"I can do that," he agreed. "Not a problem."

She watched him lift the cup to his lips and take a sip. In spite of everything, she felt a little shiver of awareness at the knowledge they'd soon be alone again, working together.

In a room where a murder had been committed, she reminded herself, an entirely different shiver quaking through her. And that was all that mattered.

THE UPSTAIRS HALLWAY had been quiet and still when Tom had left his room. He'd expected the others were still in bed, and after the night they'd had, he'd figured they'd stay there for hours. But it was only five minutes later when the others began to appear, congregating in the dining room.

Alex was the first to arrive, peering blearily around the room. "Coffee?" he blurted out when he spotted Tom.

Tom pointed to the carafes—one regular, one decaf—Meredith had set out on a side table. "The one on the left is the one you want."

Scott and Rachel followed soon after, then Jessica, with Greg close behind. No one looked particularly happy to be up, and everyone seemed nervous, glancing around the room uneasily as soon as they stepped inside.

"I wasn't expecting anyone else to be up this early," Tom told them, trying to keep his tone somewhat upbeat.

"I heard people in the hall and figured everyone was coming down," Jessica said. "I didn't want to be the only one upstairs." She plunked what looked like a heavy book-end on the table next to her plate.

"What's that?" Alex asked.

"I'm not walking around here unarmed."

"That's not a bad idea," Rachel murmured.

"I couldn't agree more," Greg said. As he said it, he set an unopened bottle of wine he'd been holding by the neck onto the table.

Tom couldn't blame them for the impulse, but the idea of everyone walking around with a weapon, nervous and ready to lash out at the slightest hint of danger, seemed like a recipe for disaster. Someone was destined to get hurt.

Then again, with a killer in the house likely intending to strike again, that was already a very real possibility.

As if she'd heard the others come in, Meredith suddenly backed through the kitchen door, carrying a tray laden with dishes. She held the door, and Ellen came through a few seconds later, pushing a cart bearing more plates. The incredible aromas Tom had smelled in the kitchen earlier began to fill the room. The others mostly began to perk up slightly at the arrival of the food.

Tom rose to his feet. "Can I help you with that?" he asked Meredith, already starting to push away from the table.

She gave her head a firm shake. "No. I have it. You're a guest here. Thank you, though."

She gently eased the tray onto the table and immediately began to unload the dishes. Settling back in his chair, Tom watched her work with a growing sense of admiration. She moved quickly, graciously tending to each of her guests in turn. Her smile remained in place, her tone courteous and upbeat. There was no hint of the tension she had to be feeling given the circumstances. Looking at her, no one would have believed anything was wrong.

Everyone began reaching for the dishes. All but one, Tom suddenly noticed. Jess didn't reach for the food, surveying the meal, Ellen and Meredith with open suspicion.

"Something wrong, Jess?" he asked.

Every eye in the room moved toward her. Jessica raised her chin, staring straight at Ellen. "Are we sure it's safe to eat?"

Everyone froze. Tom sensed a few of them glancing down at their plates.

Ellen's smile didn't waver, but Tom didn't miss the hint of outrage that flashed in her eyes as Jess's meaning hit home. It quickly disappeared as she raised a brow and met Jess's stare. "If I'd wanted to poison you folks, I could have done it last night at dinner and saved myself all this trouble, now couldn't I?" Without waiting for a response, she spun away and swept into the kitchen.

The uncomfortable silence remained in her wake. Jess didn't look remotely chagrined, clamping her lips together in a tight line. No one seemed to know what to do.

Finally Tom reached out and plucked a biscuit from the basket in front of him. Lifting it to his mouth, he took a big—and pointed—bite and began chewing. "Tastes good to me," he said, not having to fake his enthusiasm.

Within moments, Greg picked up the dish of eggs. The others soon followed. Finally even Jess reached for a piece of toast. It wasn't long before they were all eating.

Tom met Meredith's eyes, gratitude shining in her gaze. He nodded shortly, trying to ignore the feeling that filled his chest at her thankfulness. As reasonable as he knew it was for the wedding party to suspect the staff—and vice versa—they couldn't afford to turn on each other. It would only make things more unbearable—and dangerous—around here. And Ellen was right. If she *was* the killer, why would she have gone through the trouble of dragging the body into the hall to terrify them, only to poison them all the next morning? No, whoever the killer was—though he wasn't ruling her out completely—that person was playing a longer game.

"By the way," Meredith announced once everyone was eating. "I wanted to let everyone know that I was thinking of going through Haley's room and seeing if I can find any clues to indicate who might have wanted to hurt her and why. I just didn't want anyone to be surprised if you hear us in there."

Everyone fell quiet, glancing at one another. Tom waited for someone to comment or offer any objection.

"Us?" Alex asked.

"I asked Tom to come with me to videotape the room and document where everything is before I move anything."

"Sounds like you have it all figured out," Alex said in a tone Tom couldn't quite read.

"Did anyone think of any ideas why someone might have wanted to hurt Haley?" Meredith asked.

Everyone looked around the table, seemingly hoping someone else would provide the answer. No one did.

Tom had spent much of last night considering the question himself, trying to think of the slightest reason anyone might have to kill Haley, going over every interaction he'd witnessed since they had assembled at the airport. But he wasn't convinced he was the best one to figure it out. He'd been away from the group too long. Anything could have happened within the past seven years that he would have no idea about.

Still, his natural inclination was to believe that none of these people was capable of killing anyone, let alone a friend. That left him trying to figure out who else it could be—and why.

The only other people at Sutton Hall were Rick and Ellen, neither of whom he could read all that well. He didn't know enough about either of them to guess why one of them might have killed Haley. If it was one of them, the motive likely had nothing to do with Haley herself and involved something secret on their part. The fact that the knife used hadn't come from Sutton Hall didn't necessarily mean anything. If someone in the wedding party could have brought it here with them, one of the staff could have brought it, too.

If he could figure out the motive, it might help him discover who was responsible. It seemed strange that Haley would be killed here of all places, where another wedding had also ended in murder. It seemed the killer had decided to take advantage of the mansion's history. Or, he thought with a frown, was the mansion itself the connection?

He slowly raised his eyes to look at Meredith. This wedding business was hers. She was the reason anyone had come here in the first place. And two of those weddings had led to murder. He knew she was no murderer. Even if she hadn't been with him when Haley had likely been killed, he remembered the devastation on her face last night. No, she wasn't the killer, but...

"Maybe it's not about Haley," he said slowly. "Maybe it's about Meredith."

Meredith flinched, just as every eye in the room turned to her. "Me?"

"Maybe somebody has a grudge against you…." As he said it, his gaze automatically slid toward Jessica.

Jess's mouth fell open, leaving no doubt she'd caught his meaning. "Are you talking about me?"

"You seem to know a lot about Meredith and Brad. How exactly is it that you know so much? Have you been talking to him?"

She clamped her lips together in a thin line. From her expression, she didn't want to answer, but her reaction was enough of one.

"Well?" Alex prodded.

"We had coffee a few weeks ago," she sniffed.

"Exactly how long have the two of you been in touch?" Tom asked.

"We ran into each other a few months ago, that's all."

"And what did Brad have to say about Meredith and the fact that she owns this place?"

She grimaced, clearly indicating that whatever he'd said, it hadn't been good. "He's not her biggest fan," Jessica admitted delicately.

"Enough that he was pleased to hear how things went badly here before?"

She bit the inside of her cheek, her silence telling. The answer was yes. Brad Jackson had relished everything his ex-wife had been through.

"You can hardly blame him," Jess said. "After what she said about him, he has every right to enjoy what's happened to her. It's karma."

His eyes narrowing, Tom surveyed her, trying to figure out just how deep her spite ran. "You're obviously on his side. If he did want to do something to hurt Meredith, how far would you be willing to go to help him?"

Her jaw swung loose. "You can't honestly believe I would kill Haley!"

He paused. No, he admitted, deep down he didn't believe that. "Maybe not. But where is Brad right now?"

"Back in Chicago."

"You're sure about that?" he prodded.

She blinked. "Well, no, but I assume so."

"What are you suggesting, Tom?" Scott asked.

Honestly, he wasn't really sure. But Haley seemed like the last person who would have been killed by one of her longtime friends. And if Brad was holding a grudge, who knew how far he would go? He did already have a history of violence against women....

Even as he considered the idea, Tom had to wonder whether he was letting his reflexive dislike and anger toward the man affect his thinking. "Just exploring every possibility."

Jessica slammed her hand against the table. "I'm tired of hearing a good man insulted like this. It might make for good TV, Tom, but it has nothing to do with reality. He didn't do anything to *her*—" she jerked her head toward Meredith "—and he certainly didn't have anything to do with Haley's murder."

To her credit, Meredith didn't say anything to defend herself. She simply stared at Jessica, long and steadily, before pointedly looking away. The clear message was that she didn't need to defend herself. They were her experiences. She knew what had happened better than Jessica did.

As if recognizing the unspoken point, Jessica's face reddened further with suppressed anger. She looked at Rachel. "I hate this. I wish you'd never brought us here."

Rachel offered no disagreement. She lowered her eyes

to her plate, her expression uncomfortable and more than a little guilty.

"Why *did* you bring us here?" Alex asked. "Why did you have to get married here of all places?"

Rachel waved a hand around the room defensively. "Look at this place. It's amazing. Who wouldn't want to get married somewhere like this?"

"Anyone who's heard what happened here?" Alex suggested. "I have to believe most people would have canceled their weddings after that murder. Right, Meredith?"

"Most of the other weddings were canceled," Meredith admitted.

"'Most?'" Alex echoed.

"All," Meredith confirmed after a beat.

"But not you," Alex said to Rachel. "You still dragged us all up here. Why?"

Rachel hesitated, obviously struggling to think of a response.

It was Jessica who answered. "She said she thought it would make her wedding even more special," Jess interjected. "She didn't think anyone else would want to get married here after what happened, so she'd get to have the only wedding here. And even if there were other weddings, hers would still be the first."

"Jess!" Rachel snapped.

"Well, it's true," Jessica shot back. "If we all get killed, at least we'll know why."

"So I wanted my wedding to be special," Rachel sniped. "What bride doesn't?"

"Brides who don't want their wedding parties to be murdered?" Greg suggested wryly.

"No one else is going to be murdered," Tom said firmly. "If we all watch out for each other, and figure out who's responsible for killing Haley, we should be able to get through this."

The statement was met with silence, skepticism heavy in the air. Still, he figured the fact that no one voiced their doubt out loud had to be considered a positive.

"How long does it look like we're going to be here?" Rachel asked.

"It's still snowing," Tom said. "We won't be able to start digging out until it stops. If it takes a couple of days, I'm guessing it would be Monday or even Tuesday before we can get out."

Today was Friday, a grim fact that seemed to settle over the table like a lead weight. Monday couldn't possibly have seemed further away.

"So what are we supposed to do until then?" Jessica asked, her tone unusually subdued.

No one seemed to have an answer for that. The possibilities of what could happen in the meantime were too grim and terrifying.

It was Greg who finally responded, lifting his flask yet again. When he spoke, there was no humor in his voice, his tone ironically sober.

"We survive."

Chapter Eight

"Hey, Meredith."

Meredith looked up from the table where she'd begun to collect the breakfast dishes. Most of the room had cleared, but Alex lingered on the other side of the table. She suddenly felt the emptiness of the room much more strongly, keenly aware that she was completely alone with him.

She did her best to shake off the feeling. Even if he was a threat, they had the massive table separating them. If he tried anything, she could run before he made it around the thing. And Ellen was just in the kitchen behind her if she called out. "Hi, Alex. Is there something I can do for you?"

"We didn't really get a chance to talk yesterday," he said, gracing her with a smile. "I thought it would be nice to catch up with an old colleague from the *Daily,* but I wasn't sure if you remembered me from back then."

Her nervousness eased as she picked up on his meaning. "Of course," she said, unable to hide her surprise. "How could I forget a fellow *Daily* staffer? If anything, I would have thought you didn't remember me."

Back in school, they'd both worked on the college paper. But while he'd been a star reporter, she'd been a cartoonist, drawing satirical cartoons and her own strip. It had been the best part of her college experience. She'd loved to draw, and with her cartoons, she'd had a chance to give voice to the thoughts and ideas she'd seldom had the guts to out loud. Even though she doubted most of the student body could have identified her on sight, she knew they were aware of her cartoons. Sometimes she'd hear people talking about them, and it hadn't mattered that they didn't know her. Knowing they'd enjoyed her work had been the best feeling imaginable.

She hadn't really socialized with the rest of the paper's staff, working on her own and submitting her stuff directly to her editor. The few times she'd attended one of the staff parties, she'd mostly found herself standing against a wall, feeling out of place and uncomfortable. Though she'd known who Alex was, she was sure they'd never spoken to each other, and she never would have thought he knew who she was.

"Hey, your stuff was some of the most popular material in the paper," he said heartily. "I admit it took me a second to put it together, but I finally did. Do you still draw?"

Meredith didn't let her smile slip. "Not really."

As though caused by the thought, she felt a twinge in her right hand and flexed her fingers to try to alleviate the pain. Her hand had been broken a few years ago—*Brad,* she thought, reminded of the conversation earlier—and it hadn't healed correctly. Now it hurt to grip a pencil for too long, but sometimes she found herself sketching, doing her best to ignore the pain until she no longer could, unable to resist the urge. The instinct—the need—to draw was still deeply ingrained within her, even in her broken bones.

"Aw, that's too bad. So listen," he said, his mood and tone abruptly shifting. "I was thinking, you mind if I join you and Tom while you go through Haley's room? I probably know the group better than either of you and might catch a clue you wouldn't. It couldn't hurt to have an extra pair of eyes, right?"

So this was what he really wanted, Meredith thought wryly. All that catching up had simply been a way to ease into her good graces and get what he wanted.

She shouldn't have been surprised. In college, he'd earned a reputation as someone who'd do anything to get a story. That had continued in his professional career. He'd quickly made a name for himself, winning awards, admiration and more than a few enemies with a number of hard-hitting exposés and investigative pieces. He seemed to relish exposing wrongdoing and fighting for the little guy.

She had a feeling she knew what drove him, she thought with a pang of sympathy. Everyone at school had known his story. Sophomore year he'd been in an accident, struck by a hit-and-run driver while he was walking just off-campus. He'd been in bad shape, broken one leg badly and suffered several other injuries. He'd been forced to miss half a semester, but he'd fought his way back, managing to graduate in time with everyone else. More important, the accident seemed to have given him an extra motivation. The driver who'd struck him had never been caught, and he'd become a much tougher reporter, turning into the relentless force who wouldn't let anything stop him from breaking a story.

And now he was in the middle of a story. Meredith did her best to hide her discomfort. Even though she probably knew him better than anyone else in the wedding party, she still didn't know him particularly well. Certainly not well enough to trust him.

And she didn't, she acknowledged. There was something off-putting about the eagerness in his expression, as though he couldn't wait to get into the dead woman's room and go through her things.

She forced a smile. "Actually, I think it would be best to limit the number of people who go in the room, since it is a crime scene. I'd like to try to disturb it as little as possible. I'm sure you understand."

His expression froze, but she didn't miss the flash of anger in his eyes. From the way his lips thinned into an angry line, he didn't understand, or at least he didn't like it. He looked like he wanted to argue the point. Not that he had any grounds to. It was her house and her call, something he must have realized, since he'd asked her instead of suggesting it to Tom. She was the owner of Sutton Hall. Tom was the video expert. If anyone was going into the room, it was going to be the two of them.

"Sure," he said, smiling faintly. "I understand. No problem."

With a tight nod, he turned and walked from the room. Meredith watched him go, noticing the small, barely perceptible hitch in his step. It seemed he still had a slight limp from the accident he'd had in college. In spite of everything, she felt a twinge of sympathy. She knew all too well how the effects of some injuries could linger—physically and emotionally.

Troubled, she went over the encounter in her head as she continued clearing the table. She couldn't help wondering if there wasn't more to his offer, a different reason he wanted access to the room than to help with the investigation. Was he hoping to write about this experience? She supposed it made sense, even if it seemed a little distasteful to be considering it so soon. Or was there something else to it....

The kitchen door swung open and Ellen stepped into the room. "All done? I can take that."

Meredith glanced over to discover she'd fully loaded the cart without realizing it. The table was clear. "Thanks, Ellen," she said, allowing the cook to take the cart. "I should probably go check on everyone." She suspected more than a few of them had headed back to bed for a nap at the very least, but her encounter with Alex had left her more curious to see what she might find in Haley's room. She should track down Tom and see if he was ready to go through it.

After holding the swinging door to let Ellen push the cart into the kitchen, Meredith stepped out of the dining room and into the hall. She drew up short when she saw two figures standing near the end where it opened up into the main foyer.

Rachel and Jessica stood close together, heads bent in conversation. They were speaking in hushed tones, their voices whispers Meredith couldn't make out from where she stood. She could still catch the anger in them, their tones harsh and insistent as the women glared at each other, their faces dark and tense.

Meredith wasn't sure whether she should duck back into the dining room before they noticed her. The choice was taken out of her hands an instant later when Jessica suddenly looked up, her eyes locking on Meredith.

She abruptly straightened. Noticing she'd lost Jessica's attention, Rachel glanced over and saw Meredith, too.

Meredith watched the anger drain from their faces. Before she could say anything, Jessica quickly spun away and disappeared into the main hall. A moment later, Rachel followed, ducking her head and walking away.

What was that about? Meredith had to wonder. A continuation of their earlier argument at breakfast?

She didn't know, and more than anything she suddenly wished she did.

STANDING IN HALEY'S room was no more comfortable in the light of day than it had been the night before. Even with the light streaming through the window, the scene was unrelentingly grim.

Mostly because the blood in the middle of the floor was impossible to avoid no matter where Meredith looked.

As she had when he'd documented the body, she stood out of the way while Tom captured the room on camera. Lingering just inside the door, she studied the space. She was glad they'd chosen to put Haley's body in another room. This task would be even more difficult than it already was if they had to do it with the body lying there, its presence as unavoidable as the blood.

Folding her arms over her chest, Meredith fought her unease. There wasn't much to go through, she noted, wondering if they were wasting their time. Haley had only brought two pieces of luggage with her. Both were unzipped and looked to still be full, as if she hadn't unpacked them. Maybe she hadn't had time to, Meredith thought with a pang. On the top of the desk was a laptop and a few manila folders, the bag she'd brought them in sitting on the desk chair.

The wardrobe against the wall opposite the bed was slightly ajar. Meredith watched as Tom opened it, revealing only two items hung inside. One was the coat Haley had been wearing yesterday when she'd arrived.

The other was a bridesmaid's dress, still encased in a plastic bag.

Meredith couldn't take her eyes off it, even after Tom moved on to record something else. She imagined Haley hanging up the dress, thinking about when she'd put it on in a few days. And now she never would.

The way no one might ever dress for that wedding, she thought. She hadn't asked Scott and Rachel about their plans for the wedding, the issue somehow insignificant in the midst of everything else. She assumed they'd decided to cancel it, if they'd given any thought to it at all. There didn't seem to be any way the wedding could go on. Not with one of the bridesmaids now dead.

Not with a killer on the loose.

"Done," Tom said, drawing her attention back to him.

She watched him lower the camera to his side, stopping to face her. "Where do you want to get started?" he asked.

"I was just thinking there isn't that much, is there? Just her bags and what's on the desk."

"Do you want to start with the bags? Get it over with?"

"Sure." It was as good an idea as any. Meredith quickly checked through the luggage, finding nothing but the expected clothes. Not feeling all that comfortable going through a dead woman's clothes, she finished as soon as possible, leaving the bags where they'd been.

They moved to the desk. Sitting on top of it were the laptop and manila folders she'd noticed earlier. Tom reached for the bag on the desk chair, looking inside to see if it contained anything.

Picking up one of the folders, Meredith opened it to find a small stack of photographs. She lifted them out to look closer, recognizing several of the faces in the top one. "It looks like she brought pictures of all of you in college."

She sensed him glance over her shoulder. "Yesterday at dinner Haley said she'd planned a slideshow. I think she'd intended to display it for everyone tonight or tomorrow. She asked me if I'd help her set it up."

His voice had softened as he spoke, the words tinged with regret.

"If she did, maybe she had it on her laptop," Meredith said, pointing to it on the desk. "These must be extras she printed out for people to look at, or ones that weren't digitized."

"I wonder if it's worth checking her computer to see if there's anything on it...." Opening it, he began to boot the device. She watched his fingers move over the keys, her gaze drifting over his hands. He had beautiful wrists, she registered, strong, solid, lightly dusted with fine blond hairs....

It hit her what she was doing and she almost shook herself. *Get a grip already.* She was actually ogling the man's *wrists.*

She quickly looked down at the pictures in her hands, focusing on the image on top. Four young women with their arms around one another, heads pressed together, posed for the camera, their smiles wide and beaming. Three of them were easily recognizable. Rachel was second from the left, with Haley and then Jessica to her right. The fourth face wasn't familiar.

"Password protected," she heard Tom say.

Meredith held up the photograph for him to see. "Who's this?" she asked, pointing to the face on the far left.

A hint of sadness entered his eyes. "That's Kim Logan, the fourth member of Rachel's group. They shared an apartment off-campus the last two years of college. The four of them were as close as Scott, Greg, Alex and I were. It made kind of a nice symmetry when we used to hang out. But that ended when Scott and Rachel broke up. Rachel didn't want to see Scott anymore, and they each kept their respective friends."

Meredith looked at him in surprise. "Scott and Rachel broke up?"

Tom nodded. "Halfway through senior year."

"What happened?"

"I never really knew," Tom admitted, reaching for one of the other folders. "All I know is, when we got back from winter break, Rachel ended things with him. Scott never wanted to go into it, and I didn't try to push him into talking about it. That's not what guys do. I just tried to be there for him as a friend, which basically meant talking about anything else to keep his mind off it."

"But they got back together," Meredith noted.

"Last year, I guess. They ran into each other in the city, and evidently it was like old times. They started seeing each other again, and suddenly they were engaged. I actually found out from Scott that they were getting married before I heard they'd gotten back together."

"So it was fast," Meredith mused.

"Very. But it must have been right. Watching them the past couple days, it's like no time has passed at all. Whatever happened between them, or whatever made Rachel break up with him, they seem to have gotten past it."

"I wonder what it was."

He shrugged. "Me, too, but I figure it's none of my business. Kind of hard to imagine Scott doing anything, though. He was always kind of a pushover when it came to her. Some things really haven't changed. After all, it's why we're here now. Rachel wanted to get married here, even though it's so far from where everybody lives. As usual, she got her way."

So many things had brought them to this point. If Scott and Rachel hadn't gotten back together, would any of this be happening now? Or if Rachel hadn't wanted everyone to come here?

Meredith studied Kim Logan's face. She didn't remember her, but that wasn't a surprise. She hadn't exactly moved in this group's social circle. She hadn't moved in any social circle, at least not until she'd met Brad and been reluctantly tolerated in his. "What was she like? Kim?"

"Kim was the wild one of their group. When we would all hang out, she and Greg were pretty tight. That should give you some idea what she was like. She liked to party as much as he did, and could match him shot for shot. I'm not sure what she ended up doing after college. The others said she died a few months ago, and Jessica made a comment about how she wouldn't have been invited anyway. I'm guessing she and Rachel had some kind of falling-out."

It was so sad, Meredith thought, looking at the two of them in the picture. They looked really close. All of them did, the tightness of their bond visibly apparent in the image. And now two of them were dead. Half of their group was gone.

She forced herself to move on to the next picture, then the rest. There were more group shots of the four girls, then some that started to include the guys. Everyone looked so young, she thought with a twinge.

And there was Tom. Not the Tom who stood beside her, but the Tom she remembered so well from those old fantasies. He looked so young. She could see what she'd seen in him back then, yet he'd improved so much with age. He really had only been a boy then. Now he was every bit a man.

Forcing herself to look away, Meredith handed him the stack of photographs to go through in case he spotted anything in them. Wiping her hands on her slacks, she scanned the space. That really was it. Everything else in the room was here when Haley arrived.

It was a good thing she'd turned down Alex's offer to "help," she thought. There was barely enough here for her and Tom to go through. She didn't know what a third person could have done.

The thought reminded her of her earlier encounter with him and all the questions she'd had. "What can you tell me about Alex?" Meredith asked carefully.

"Why do you ask?" Tom said, a trace of wariness in his tone.

"After breakfast he asked me if he could come in here

with us and look around, see if he could help find some clues."

Tom relaxed imperceptibly. "Well, that makes sense. He is a reporter. He's used to asking questions and conducting investigations. I'm not surprised he would want to get involved in the search for the killer."

"I know," she said. "It makes sense. But there was something about the way he asked, almost like he was too eager. I had to wonder if there was another reason he wanted to get in here."

"He can be a little intense," Tom admitted. "I'm sure that's a good quality for his line of work, but it can turn people off, too. He can come on a little strong, but he's a good guy. He's one of the most loyal friends anyone could want."

Meredith figured she would reserve judgment on whether Alex was really a good guy. "What kind of relationship did he and Haley have?"

Tom paused for a moment. "Actually, I think he liked her back in school," he said thoughtfully. "But nothing ever came of it. I don't think she was interested." He shook his head. "I'd forgotten about that."

"Do you remember if he was upset about it?"

"I doubt it. I hate to say it, but he was probably used to it. Back then, Alex never had much luck with girls. He was pretty awkward with them. It was that intensity thing. He would always get really serious and want to talk about issues and stuff like that. He seems a lot smoother now from what I can tell." He smiled slightly. "Greg was always the ladies' man of our group. And Scott was all about Rachel. Even after they broke up, he didn't date much through the rest of college."

"What about you?" she asked without thinking. "You weren't a ladies' man?"

Almost as soon as she asked the question, she wished she hadn't. She sounded a little *too* interested.

If he noticed, he didn't show it. He chuckled lightly, a touch of self-deprecation in the sound. "Not really. I dated a few girls, but nothing too serious. What Scott and Rachel had was nice, but I really wasn't looking for anything like that. And I never met anybody who tempted me to change my mind."

"You didn't want to settle down," she said, more of an observation than a question.

"No," he agreed with a small smile. "I grew up in a small town in Minnesota. I wanted to get out there, see the world. Experience what's out there."

"And you did," she said, matching his smile. She had to admire that about him. He was a man who'd had a dream and managed to fulfill it. How many people could say that at any age, let alone before the age of thirty?

"So what's next for you?" she asked. "What do you want to do now?"

"I'm still figuring that out," he admitted. "What about you? Do you keep in touch with people from school?"

She shrugged halfheartedly. "Not really. I didn't have a lot of close friends back then. I guess I was kind of a loner. When I started seeing Brad, I kind of got swept up in his group, and after we graduated and got married, I lost touch with the few people I was close to."

"How long were you married?"

"Four years," she said softly.

"So you got married right out of college?"

"We lived together for a year first." She frowned. "Did you really mean what you suggested at breakfast? You think Brad could be responsible?"

"I don't know," he said. "Part of it was just trying to

think of who might want to hurt *you*. Part of it was being tired of hearing about him and just plain not liking the guy."

"You don't even know him," Meredith pointed out.

He looked at her, his expression solemn. "He hurt you," he said gravely. "That's reason enough."

A curious warmth rolled through her at both the seriousness of the words and the intensity of his expression. It didn't sound like he was simply being polite. It almost sounded personal.

"But you tell me," he continued. "You know him better than I do. Do you think he could be involved in this?"

Meredith frowned, considering the question. She knew Brad had been angry about the divorce, in spite of everything he'd done. It was one reason she'd been glad to get away from Chicago, needing the physical distance between them. And she knew better than anyone he was capable of violence when he was angry. But to murder an innocent person just to get back at her? If anything it seemed more likely that he would take his anger out on her directly.

Of course, there was a time she never would have believed he'd ever hurt her. She was both an expert at knowing what Brad was capable of, and someone with a history of underestimating him.

"I don't know," she finally said. "It seems like a lot of trouble to go to in order to hurt me, instead of simply coming after me directly."

"He must have been pretty bitter about your divorce, and still is, if he's complaining about it over a year later."

"He was," she said quietly. "He tried to fight the divorce. At first, he swore that he loved me and he'd change. And when that didn't work, he got furious and said that we'd made those vows until death. But all that did was remind me exactly why I needed to get away from him."

"I'm glad you did," he said.

"*If* I did," she pointed out. "If he's not somehow involved in this—"

He suddenly frowned, his brow furrowing and eyes sliding away from hers. She started to drift off in midsentence, about to ask what was wrong. He suddenly twirled his finger, prompting her to continue, and mouthed, *Keep talking.*

Not understanding, she still tried to comply, scrambling to pick up her earlier train of thought. "Hopefully the phone lines will be up soon and we can contact the police. Even if they can't get through due to the storm, they should be able to check where he is…"

She continued talking as he slowly, cautiously made his way to the door, leaning toward it with one ear, as though he was listening for something. Which was exactly what he was doing, she realized. When he was almost there, he slowly reached out to grasp the knob…

The door abruptly swung inward, slamming right into him.

With a curse, he reeled backward. Meredith stopped in shock, her monologue forgotten, then lurched toward him. By the time she did, he managed to steady himself. Lunging forward, he grabbed the door and ripped it open, bursting out into the hall. His face dark with anger, he checked in both directions.

Meredith stepped into the hall behind him, doing the same. There was no one in sight. The corridor was empty, all the doors along it closed.

"Did you see anyone?" she asked.

"No," he said tersely. "Whoever it was either managed to get into one of the rooms or made it to the stairs."

Meredith eyed the closed doors. Haley's room was roughly in the middle of the ones where she'd placed the wedding party. Scott and Rachel's room was one door down on one side to give them some privacy, with Jessica's next door on the other side and Tom, Greg and Alex across the hall. Whoever had been there could have easily escaped to one of the rooms, or even the staircase, which wasn't far, by the time Tom had recovered and made it into the hall.

"What do you think they were doing there?" she asked. "Listening to us?"

"I'm sure they were," he confirmed. "And they didn't want us to know."

"How *did* you know?"

"I thought I heard the floor creak outside the door. Now we just have to wonder how long they were there."

And whether whoever it was had heard anything important. Meredith doubted it. She and Tom had simply been speculating. Yet whoever it was still hadn't wanted them to know who'd been listening, going far enough to lash out to prevent them from catching him or her.

Meredith looked up at Tom, noticing the red spot on his forehead where the door had slammed into him. Cringing, she reached up without thinking to brush her fingers over the spot. "Does it hurt?"

As soon as her fingertips made contact with his skin, she froze. Her eyes shot to his to find him watching her, his deep blue gaze intent and unyielding. She couldn't tell what he was thinking, couldn't read the emotion in those depths. Everything in her wanted to keep trying, unable to bring herself to look away.

It occurred to her she should drop her hand, even as she registered the warmth and smoothness of his skin against hers. It was rude to just reach out and touch him like this. She had no right.

But he didn't offer a word of objection, simply watching her, his expression inscrutable.

"Not too much," he said softly, the sound of his voice washing over her skin. "I'll be fine."

"Good." Her voice sounding tight to her ears, she quickly pulled her hand away and glanced back at the room. "Is there anything else we need to do in here?"

She sensed him follow her gaze. "I don't think so. I think we checked everything there is. Do you want to check the rest of the house? Just to be safe?"

It wasn't a bad idea. She doubted there was anyone unknown to her hiding in the house. But reality said she couldn't be absolutely certain of that without checking. And given everything that had happened so far, they couldn't afford to take any chances.

Chapter Nine

"There's no one here," Tom concluded.

"I don't think so, either," Meredith agreed. He couldn't tell if what he heard in her voice was relief or simply exhaustion.

Either one would make sense. They'd spent hours going through Sutton Hall from top to bottom, finally winding up here, in the ballroom in the west wing.

They stood in the middle of the ballroom floor, dwarfed by the massive space that stretched two stories high and half the length of the wing. On one side of the room was a stage they'd already checked. There was a skylight high overhead and windows covered nearly half of the outside wall. All that could be seen beyond them was an impenetrable whiteness. He thought he could hear the faint sound of the wind howling in the distance. Or maybe it was just the emptiness of the room echoing around them, he thought, his skin suddenly prickling with unease.

"There are certainly a lot of hiding places around here," he noted.

"I guess that's the downside of how big it is."

"This place really is incredible, though," Tom said, leaning back to scan his surroundings.

"It is, isn't it?" Meredith said, a wistful, almost resigned note in her voice.

Tom glanced over at her. Her expression was heavy with sadness. It had to be impossible for her not to remember how this amazing place had been touched by so much ugliness.

It was a shame, too. He wasn't exaggerating—Sutton Hall really was extraordinary, he thought, craning his head to peer up into the high ceilings. From the massive ballroom to the tower bedrooms, the library to the atrium, the place was more like an actual castle than anything he ever would have expected to find in this country—or outside of a storybook. There were moments when they'd come upon a sight so amazing he'd nearly forgotten the purpose for their search and simply wanted to take in his surroundings.

Unfortunately, reality had always returned soon enough, reminding him exactly why they were doing this.

"I'm guessing you weren't planning on using this space for Scott and Rachel."

"No," Meredith agreed. "It seemed a bit much with only the six of you. I know Rachel was excited to see the ballroom, but we were going to use more intimate spaces for the wedding events. The atrium in the back of the manor seemed like a good choice, and the library is lovely."

"Still, seems like a shame not to be able to put this to use."

She nodded. "It does. When I first came up with the idea of holding weddings here, I imagined all these big events that could really take advantage of such a magnificent space. But most of the weddings that planned to come here were smaller, like Scott and Rachel's. In retrospect, it does make sense. It would be harder to get a large group of people to travel all the way to such a remote location." She gave her head a small shake. "I guess this really was a bad idea."

Before he could say anything she started to turn away. "I think we're done here."

They made their way out of the room, Meredith stopping to lock the doors behind them. Despite the massive amount of territory they'd covered, there were no doubt places they hadn't reached. It would likely take days to conduct a thorough search of every inch of Sutton Hall. Even so, they hadn't detected any signs there was anyone else on the premises who wasn't supposed to be here. For the time being, and without any evidence otherwise, Tom was inclined to believe that meant there really wasn't anyone else here.

Which meant the killer was most likely someone they were already aware of. Either one of the members of Meredith's staff—

Or one of his old friends.

A sense of resignation settled over him at the thought. He still didn't want to believe it was possible. But the longer he thought about it, the more he knew he had to.

"Can I ask you something?" Tom asked as they made their way down the corridor toward the front foyer.

"Sure."

"Why didn't you ask Rick to help us with the search?"

A guilty flush colored her cheeks. "I wasn't sure if I should. He's pretty much had the run of the place for the past several days, so if there was somebody here, he should have already known about it."

"And if there was somebody here, that would mean he was keeping it from you, and probably was involved with that person being here in the first place."

"Exactly," she allowed. "Now that it looks like there's no one else here, I hate that I didn't automatically trust him, but I didn't think I could afford to. Not if there was even a chance…"

"But you trust me?"

She glanced over at him, her gaze direct and unguarded. "I do," she said simply.

Her unquestioned confidence struck him hard. A mixture of awe and pride and pleasure like nothing he'd ever felt before filled him in the face of her approval.

They reached the main staircase in the front hall. As they descended the stairs, Tom glanced up at the portrait hanging on the wall above the landing halfway down. He'd noticed it before but hadn't paid much attention to it. It depicted a couple, a bride and groom on their wedding day from the looks of it. The image seemed to loom over him and Meredith, oppressive and unsettling. Given everything that had happened in the past twenty-four hours, it was an eerie reminder of exactly what had brought them all here—and of Scott and Rachel's wedding that wouldn't take place.

Meredith must have noticed his attention. "That's the previous owner of Sutton Hall, Jacob Sutton, and his wife, Kathleen, on their wedding day," she explained.

"Is that where you got the idea to hold weddings here?" he asked, coming to a stop on the landing.

"Actually, yes."

Tom took in the smiling faces of the bride and groom, the joy seeming to radiate from them and out of the portrait. It was impossible not to think of Scott and Rachel. Even when they finally did manage to get married, they likely wouldn't be able to take as much joy in it as this couple had. The moment would inevitably be colored by what had happened here.

"They look happy," he observed.

"From what I was told, they were. For a few years at least."

Tom didn't miss the note of sadness that had entered her voice. "What happened to them?"

"She was killed in a car accident about five years into

their marriage. He never got over it. He lived the rest of his life here alone."

Tom studied the face of the fresh-faced groom in the portrait. He really did look happy, his hand clasping his bride's, his smile broad and beaming. Tom tried to imagine him as an older man, tragic and alone in this massive mansion. He couldn't do it, or maybe he just didn't want to. "That's really sad," he murmured, the words feeling inadequate to convey how true it was.

"Yes, it is," Meredith said softly. "When we first came here and I heard their story, I actually thought it was incredibly romantic, the idea of a love that didn't die even though one of the people in it had. But now I think about him in this huge house, shut away from everyone and everything, and it just seems like a waste. I doubt Kathleen would have wanted him to live like that. Not if she truly loved him."

"It's almost like he was hiding from the world," Tom said.

It was only an idle observation. He wasn't entirely sure why he'd said it at all. But it seemed to strike a chord in her. He glanced over in time to see her wince, her expression tightening as she slowly lowered her eyes.

And he understood, a burst of sorrow shafting through him.

Is that what you're *doing here, Meredith Sutton?* he wondered, his gut clenching. *Hiding?*

He couldn't really blame her. After what she'd been through, withdrawing from the world probably would have seemed like a relief. Maybe she'd needed that, needed the time and space to recover. Maybe she hadn't even known that was what she was doing, though, from her reaction, she seemed to be considering the possibility now.

Seeing the sadness on her face, he wished he hadn't said it. "Or maybe he just didn't feel the need to leave," Tom said, striving to lighten the tone. "This place is pretty amazing. Who would want to leave if they didn't have to?"

She forced an unconvincing smile. "I'm sure you've seen some amazing places with your job."

"That's true. But this place is certainly something special."

"That it is."

"What about you?" he asked, still hoping to distract her, if only for a moment. "Did you ever want to travel?"

"Always," she admitted. "But after Brad and I got married, it never seemed to happen. My brother, Adam, used to travel a lot for work and he'd send me postcards and souvenirs from the places he visited. It was nice to get a little taste of those places."

"But still not the same as seeing them yourself."

"No," she conceded.

"Maybe someday you will."

"Maybe," she said, her tone noncommittal. She gave herself a little shake. "We should go. We've been away from the others for a while. I want to check on everyone."

His pulse instantly kicked into a higher gear at the comment. She had a point. It had been hours since they'd seen any of the others. Anything could have happened. "Good idea."

She quickly turned away, crossing the landing to move up the other part of the staircase that led to the east wing and their rooms.

He moved to follow her, glancing toward the front of the hall as he did. It was the middle of the day. The light coming through the front windows in the foyer should have been bright, but it wasn't. It was murky, diffuse, a reminder of the storm that engulfed them, filtering out the sun.

Tom had no trouble understanding her reluctance to discuss the future.

At the moment, they couldn't even escape this place, let alone go anywhere else.

Simply making it through the next several days seemed like enough of a goal.

REACHING THE SECOND-FLOOR landing, Meredith took in the row of closed doors that met her eyes. Everything looked calm and undisturbed, with no ugly surprises waiting in the hall this time. She hoped that was a good sign. She and Tom had been gone for hours, making their way through the house. Anything could have happened since then.

There was only one way to find out. Fighting a prickle of unease, she quickly moved to the bridal suite and knocked on the door.

The moments that passed without an immediate answer seemed to last forever, her pulse picking up every second she waited.

Finally Scott's voice came from the other side of the door. "Who is it?"

"Meredith. And Tom," she added, almost as an afterthought. Maybe his presence would alleviate any reluctance they might feel about answering the door to her.

A few seconds later, the door opened slightly. Scott peered out to confirm it was them before opening it all the way. Rachel was visible behind him, pacing the floor in the center of the room.

Meredith didn't miss the way Scott's gaze shifted between the two of them, a speculative gleam in his eyes. "Hey. What's going on?"

"I just wanted to see how you both were doing."

"How do you think we're doing?" Rachel snapped. As she voiced the question she came to a sudden stop, turning to face them. Her arms folded over her chest, she looked as if she was holding herself tightly, her face tense and pale.

"We're hanging in there," Scott answered, a hint of apology in his eyes. "We're still a bit on edge."

"It's okay," Meredith assured him. "I understand."

"We went through the house," Tom said. "There doesn't appear to be any sign of anyone else in here that we don't know about."

"So most likely it's someone we are aware of," Rachel concluded. She hesitated for an instant before adding grimly, "Someone who works here."

"I trust my staff completely," Meredith said.

"The same way you trusted the last staff who worked for you?" Rachel returned. Her tone was less spiteful than Jessica's, the question blunt and matter-of-fact, which only made it sting more.

Meredith didn't let her reaction show on her face. "More," she replied firmly.

"And I trust my friends," Rachel said without hesitation, her voice unyielding.

"Neither Ellen nor Rick had any reason to want to hurt Haley—or anyone else."

"And you think one of us did?"

"You tell me," Meredith responded without rancor. "Did either of you give any more thought to why someone would want to hurt Haley?"

"None of us would!" Rachel insisted, her voice harsh with intensity. The answer was so immediate, so absolute, that Meredith believed she meant it. She just had to wonder if it was because Rachel had seriously considered it and dismissed the possibility, or because she was refusing to consider it at all.

Meredith glanced at Scott. He gave his head a small shake. "I'm sorry. We have thought about it. I honestly don't know why anyone would have wanted to hurt her, let alone kill her."

He sounded so genuine Meredith figured she had no choice but to believe him—for now. Pressing him was unlikely to get her a different answer.

She turned her attention back to Rachel. Remembering the exchange she'd witnessed between Rachel and Jessica in the hall that morning, Meredith was tempted to mention it. But she had to wonder how honest the woman would be with her fiancé in the room. She was going to have to find some way to talk to Rachel alone. It wasn't going to be easy. It was doubtful that Scott would want to leave his bride-to-be alone with anyone else anytime soon.

Meredith managed a smile. "Well, I'm glad you're both all right. I'm sure lunch will be ready soon. I'll let you both know when it is."

"Thank you," Scott said warmly. "That sounds great."

Meredith couldn't help but be grateful for his calmness. As soon as the feeling registered, she immediately experienced a flicker of doubt. Rachel's agitation certainly made sense given the circumstances. As much as she appreciated it, Scott's calmness was the more unusual response in the face of everything that was happening. Maybe she should consider *that* suspicious....

She studied his face, trying to determine if there was something else there. She couldn't read anything in his eyes other than the openness that seemed to radiate from him.

Behind him Rachel had started to pace the room again. Meredith watched her for a moment before Scott closed the door.

She was about to move down the hall when the one of the doors slowly began to open. Her wariness growing, she watched as Jessica poked her head out an instant later. Eyes wide, she glanced in both directions. As soon as she spotted them, her gaze narrowed, the now familiar contempt entering her eyes when they landed on Meredith. Straightening, she stepped all the way out into the hallway, allowing them to see she still had that bookend clutched in her right hand.

"I see you two are still together," she noted. "What's going on?"

"I'm just checking on everybody, making sure you're holding up okay."

Jessica's mouth twisted in a sneer. "Making sure we're still alive?"

Meredith forced a smile. "That, too," she admitted. "What are you doing?"

"Going to the bathroom, since my room doesn't have one of its own," she griped. Pulling her door shut, she turned the knob to make sure it was locked. With one last look of distaste at Meredith, she started to turn away.

Meredith suddenly remembered the question she hadn't been able to ask Rachel moments ago. The bride wasn't the only one who could answer it. "Jessica?"

Her shoulders tensing, Jessica stopped and shot a glance back at them. "What?"

"When I saw you and Rachel talking this morning, you looked really upset, even angry with her. Do you mind if I ask what you were talking about?"

The woman's face flushed an angry red. "As a matter of fact, yes, I do mind."

"Really?" Tom asked. "Some might think that means you have something to hide."

"I don't care what some people think, and I definitely don't care what either of you think. It's none of your business."

"One of your best friends was murdered and the killer is still on the loose."

"This has nothing to do with that. I was just angry at her for bringing us here."

"That's all it was?" Meredith asked, unable to hide her skepticism.

"I just said so, didn't I?" Jessica snapped.

"You know, we could always ask Rachel."

Meredith had hoped to provoke a reaction out of her. Instead, the anger slowly faded from Jessica's face. She lifted her chin, her lips settling back into a smirk. Even before she spoke, Meredith understood. Whatever it was, Jessica didn't think Rachel would tell them.

"Go ahead. I don't care what you do."

Spinning on her heel, she quickly hurried down the hall away from them, dashing into the bathroom and slamming the door behind her.

The noise echoed down the hallway. Meredith let out a long, slow breath, fighting the frustration and disappointment churning in her belly. Jessica was the last person she would have expected to cooperate with her, but that didn't make her refusal any less discouraging. They needed answers—badly.

"What was that about?" Tom asked.

Meredith suddenly realized she'd never told Tom about the scene she'd witnessed. "After I cleaned up the dishes from breakfast, I saw her and Rachel talking in the hallway. Or, more accurately, it looked like she was berating Rachel, although they were too far away and speaking too low for me to hear what they were saying."

"You think it could be something related to the murder?"

"I don't know," Meredith admitted. "But given the circumstances I had to at least ask, in case there was any chance it was."

"Why didn't you ask Rachel when we saw her?"

"I wasn't sure how open she would be in front of Scott. To be honest, I don't know how much she'll admit even if he isn't there, but I have to try. Hopefully, I can get a moment alone with her soon." She looked up at him. "Unless you think she'd be more likely to talk to you."

He frowned, considering the question. "I can certainly try if I get a chance to speak with her privately. But I can't be sure she'll talk to me about it, either."

"It all might be nothing." Meredith sighed.

Unfortunately, at the moment, nothing was exactly what they had.

Chapter Ten

They found Greg in his room, though it took him several minutes to respond to their knocking. Tom was about to suggest they check for him downstairs when the door finally opened.

Greg scowled at them, bleary-eyed and disheveled, his hair sticking up on one side. Obviously they'd woken him from a nap. *Or a drunken stupor,* Tom thought.

"What is it?" Greg demanded.

"We just wanted to make sure you were okay," Tom said.

"I was fine until somebody started pounding on my door," he grumbled. "Is that all?"

"That's all," Tom murmured. "Glad you're okay."

Muttering under his breath, Greg slammed the door in their faces.

"How much do you think he's had to drink today?" Meredith asked, her voice heavy with concern.

"Too much," Tom replied.

"It might make it hard for him to defend himself if the killer comes after him," Meredith noted.

"You're right." Tom sighed. "But it's never been easy to tell him he's had enough and, under the circumstances, he probably has the best excuse he's ever had. I'll have to try to keep an eye on him." It wasn't going to be easy. He was already trying to keep an eye on Meredith. He didn't want anything to happen to her. Hell, he didn't want anything to happen to *anyone*. The fact was, he needed to be thinking about watching out for his own back, as well.

They moved on to Alex's door. This time there was no answer even after several minutes. Trying not to get concerned without reason, Tom followed Meredith downstairs to see if he was somewhere else in the house.

The living room was empty when they checked it. As they approached the kitchen, Tom heard voices coming from inside the room. Ellen and Rick, he assumed.

Following Meredith through the swinging door, he immediately saw he'd been partly right. Ellen and Rick were both in the room, Ellen standing at the kitchen island, Rick leaning against the wall nearby. But they weren't alone. Alex stood on the other side of the island facing them. The tension in the air was so thick it almost seemed harder to breathe in here. Tom came to a stop an instant before Meredith did, his senses instantly going on alert.

"Everything okay in here?" Meredith asked.

"Fine," Alex said with a smile. "We were just having a nice talk."

Neither Ellen nor Rick commented on that, the silence confirmation enough of just how nice they thought it was. Tom had no trouble understanding what had been happening here. Alex had been asking questions—more like interrogating them, Tom suspected—or at least trying to. It made sense. Not only was his life in danger as much as everyone else's, Alex was predisposed to ask questions and demand the truth. Tom hadn't been kidding when he'd told Meredith about how intense Alex could get. It wasn't surprising the cook and the handyman would be uncomfortable with him pestering them, even if their jobs required them to try to be polite.

Of course, if they were innocent, they would be uncomfortable around someone they thought could be a killer, Tom conceded.

"How's lunch coming along?" Meredith asked Ellen.

"Should be ready soon."

"Great." Meredith turned to Alex. "Maybe you'd like to go wash up?"

"That's not necessary," Alex said. "I'm not really hungry. But I will get out of your way. Good talking you," he told Rick and Ellen.

They both managed faint, polite, utterly insincere smiles.

With a nod to Tom and Meredith, he moved toward the exit, the slight limp a little more noticeable as he walked.

The sight was a painful reminder of exactly what Alex had been through, exactly why he was so dogged about seeking out answers, even beyond their current circumstances. Although Meredith hadn't let him participate in searching Haley's room, it wasn't surprising that he'd do whatever he could to get to the truth—

Suddenly Tom remembered what had happened upstairs, the person who'd been listening. Alex?

He had almost reached the door, raising his hand to push it open. Tom called out, "Hey, Alex?"

Alex stopped and glanced back.

"You weren't by any chance upstairs a few hours ago when Meredith and I were going through Haley's room, were you?"

Tom watched his face closely for any sign of guilt or avoidance. He didn't find any. Alex was adept at hiding his thoughts—probably a good quality to have in his line of work, but one Tom couldn't help but wish he didn't have at the moment.

Alex raised his eyebrows slightly. "I don't know when that was, so I couldn't say. Why?"

Because someone was eavesdropping on our conversa-tion. Was it you? Tom smiled thinly. "No reason."

Alex studied him for a long moment—wondering what he was talking about, or wondering if Tom truly suspected anything? He finally nodded shortly and pushed through the doorway.

As soon as he was gone, the tension in the room seemed to palpably ease.

"Are you both okay?" Meredith asked her staff.

Tom didn't miss the way Ellen glanced uneasily at him before answering. "Sure. He just wanted to ask some ques-tions."

"What kind of questions?" Meredith asked.

Ellen shrugged. "Did we see anything last night? Have we seen anyone else around here—"

"Did we kill that woman?" Rick added tersely.

Tom surveyed the other man, who stared back, unblink-ing. As much as he knew Meredith didn't want to believe it, he had to agree with Rachel. Ellen and Rick were the two unknowns here. It made more sense that one of them was the killer.

"I'm sure you can understand where he's coming from," Meredith said. "A friend of his was murdered. It only makes sense he'd want to try to find out who's responsible. Not to mention, Mr. Corbett is a reporter. I'm sure asking ques-tions is second nature to him."

"Yes, he mentioned that," Rick noted wryly.

"Any reason why you wouldn't want to answer his ques-tions?" Tom couldn't help asking.

The man's expression didn't change in the least. "Does anyone like being accused of murder?"

"I wouldn't know. It's never happened to me. I take it it's happened to you before?"

"Yep," Rick said. "About five minutes ago."

"Rick, I was thinking about the plow," Meredith said quickly, in an obvious attempt to change the subject. "I never asked how much experience you've had with them, or how long it might take you to hook one up to the truck."

"I've never driven one or had to hook one up to a truck before," Rick admitted. "But I have experience with a lot of different kind of vehicles. I can't say for sure until I get out there and look it over, but I'm betting I can figure it out."

"Actually, I've driven a plow before," Tom said. "My dad did it for the town where I grew up and showed me how. It's been a while, and I've never tried to attach one to a truck before, but I can help if you need it."

The handyman eyed him carefully. "I'll let you know."

"You say you have experience with vehicles? What is it you used to do before you came here?" Tom asked.

"U.S. Army. Eight years."

So he'd been right when he'd thought the man's bearing reminded him of a soldier's, Tom thought. "It's a big change from the army to handyman at a mansion in the mountains."

Rick grew quiet for a moment. "I needed a change in scenery, someplace different from what I've been doing the past eight years. Thought I'd seen enough death and suffering for one lifetime. A peaceful place in the mountains sounded pretty good."

"Considering what happened here before, I'd think Sutton Hall wouldn't be a place anyone would think of as peaceful."

A shadow passed over the man's face. Rick nodded in acknowledgment. "Guess I was counting on nothing like that happening here again. Wish I hadn't been wrong about that." He stared hard at Tom. "Any other questions?"

Tom was tempted, but out of the corner of his eye he saw Meredith clenching her fists. He'd gotten more than he expected from the man, certainly enough to think about for now. "No."

"Not going to ask me if I killed her?"

Meredith jumped in. "No one thinks—"

"Did you?" Tom asked without missing a beat.

Rick's stare never wavered. "Nope."

Tom believed him. He wasn't sure he could have said exactly why he did, and he knew he probably shouldn't just take the man at his word. And yet, he believed him. Everything in his demeanor was entirely forthright. He was either a damn good liar, or he was telling the truth. In spite of everything, Tom's gut said it was the latter. "Okay then."

"What about you?" Rick shot back.

Tom raised a brow. "What about me?"

"How do we know it wasn't you?"

"It wasn't Tom," Meredith interjected. "He was with me when the murder happened. We were here in the kitchen."

"That's right," Ellen said. "You told us that."

Tom glanced at her. There was a certain innuendo in her tone he couldn't entirely read. She looked at him, then Meredith, her lips curving slightly, before returning to her work.

"Doesn't mean he couldn't have been working with the person who really did it," Rick pointed out.

"That's ridiculous," Meredith said.

Tom couldn't help but appreciate her faith in him, but he had to give her a reality check. It might force her to remain skeptical of everyone around her.

"Is it?" he asked. He saw both Meredith and Ellen look at him in surprise, but never took his eyes from Rick. "You're right. I could be. But I'm not. I had nothing to do with Haley's death."

"You didn't have to answer that," Meredith said.

"The man answered my question. Only fair that I answered his."

"Well, he shouldn't have answered yours, either, and you shouldn't have asked it," she said stubbornly. "No one in this room is a killer."

No one acknowledged the comment. Tom never took his eyes off of the handyman. Meredith seemed to believe Rick needed to be defended against the perceived insult, but the man didn't seem insulted at all. If anything, Tom thought he saw a hint of respect in the man's eyes. He was surprised to realize the feeling was mutual.

"Lunch is almost ready," Ellen announced. "Why don't you go round everyone up?"

"That's a great idea." Meredith sighed. "Tom, do you want to come with me?" The way she said it, it was clearly an order more than a request.

He didn't argue. As much as he'd like to stay and talk to Ellen, it looked like she was much less inclined to talk. And he doubted Meredith would let him get another question out as it was. With a nod to the others, he followed her from the room.

Meredith waited until they were across the dining room—and most likely out of earshot of the kitchen—before demanding, "Are you satisfied now that he didn't do it?"

"You know I had to ask."

"Well, maybe now you'll admit you need to ask about your friends. If anything we should probably be looking at Alex."

Tom frowned. "What about him?"

"He goes on his own to interrogate two people he appears to suspect of murder? You don't find that suspicious?"

"You said it yourself. You can't blame him for wanting to ask questions."

"Alone? If he really thinks one—or both—of them is the killer, would he really try talking to them alone and unarmed? It seems more likely he's trying to divert suspicion from himself, maybe get the rest of your group to turn on Rick and Ellen."

"Alex is pretty fearless. After the car accident in college, he always said if that couldn't kill him, nothing would. I'm sure that's what makes him so good at his job. He's not afraid of anything or anybody anymore."

"Well, he should be. It's only logical given the circumstances."

The comment reminded Tom of what had happened in the kitchen just a short time ago. They'd reached the entry hall. Tom stopped at the bottom of the stairs and turned to face her. "That's something we should probably talk about."

"What's that?"

"We don't know when exactly Haley was killed. Just because I was with you when the body was found doesn't mean I couldn't have done it."

Meredith blew off the comment with a wave of her hand. "If you had done it, you would have gone back to your room, not wandered around the house. You had no way of knowing I was downstairs. It would have looked much more suspicious for you to be the only one not in your room and wandering around the house when the body was found, instead of just waiting for someone to find it and coming out and acting surprised. I just didn't feel like explaining all of that to everyone."

Her words blindsided him. She had a good point, one she'd clearly thought through—and he hadn't.

Amusement crept into her eyes. "Did you think I was just trusting you blindly? I did think about it."

Tom realized that was what he'd thought, in a way. He'd underestimated her—unfairly, as it was. He should have known she was smarter than that. She'd given him no reason to doubt her in the past twenty-four hours. He owed her an apology.

Before he could offer one, Meredith looked past him and frowned. "The living room—"

Tom glanced behind him at the doors to the room, one of which was slightly ajar. "What is it?"

"I closed the doors when we came by earlier. Is someone—"

The door suddenly burst open. Tom automatically moved in front of Meredith, just as Greg stepped into the foyer.

His head slightly lowered, it apparently took him a moment to spot them. As soon as he did, he pulled up short, peering at them in surprise. "Hello."

"What were you doing in there?" Tom asked.

Greg held up his flask, giving it a shake. "Came down for a little refill. I was in the mood for some vodka."

Of course. Tom slowly let out a breath. He sensed Meredith do the same.

"We were just coming up to tell you lunch is almost ready," Meredith said.

"Great. Guess I'll head right in then." With a nod, he strolled past them on his way to the dining room, disappearing down the side hall.

Frowning, Meredith watched him go. "You know, for a group of people who know there's a killer in the house, your friends don't seem to have any reservations about wandering around on their own."

Tom was tempted to argue that Greg couldn't be counted on to make the smartest decisions when he'd been drinking, but it really wasn't much of an argument. It didn't matter that he was inebriated or that Alex was fearless. They were putting their lives in danger, and Tom couldn't keep an eye on all of them. He was going to have to say something and hope they'd listen.

And pray their recklessness didn't cost them their lives.

Chapter Eleven

"I think it's finally starting to slow down," Rick said. He stood just outside the open kitchen door, peering up at the night sky.

"It's so dark, how can you tell?" Ellen asked.

He stepped inside, closing the door behind him, and started brushing off the flakes that had fallen on him. "Can't tell for certain, but that's what it looks like to me. And if it is over, I can try to get out to the garage tomorrow and see about hooking up the plow."

Standing on the other side of the kitchen island from Ellen, Meredith let out a slow sigh of relief. "That's great, Rick." Finally some good news.

Rick eased himself onto a seat at the kitchen table. "With any luck I'll be able to start digging out the day after tomorrow, but it'll take some time to reach the garage and the plow to begin with."

"Still, it's a start," Meredith said.

"You sure anyone's coming down for dinner?" Ellen asked. She finished tossing the salad she'd been working on for the past ten minutes, finally setting the bowl aside. "I'd hate to see all this food go to waste."

Meredith set the last of the silverware that needed to be taken out to the dining room on a tray with the plates. "I reminded everyone what time dinner was at lunch. They all said they'd be here. Besides, I'm sure they must be getting a little stir-crazy by now."

"That's true," Ellen said. She turned to check on the chicken breasts she was serving as the entrée. "I haven't seen anyone in hours. Been awfully quiet today. Even more than usual in this place. Feels unnatural somehow."

The cook was right. Meredith had felt it, too. Most of the wedding party had kept to their rooms the rest of the day. Meredith didn't know if it was to catch up on their sleep or because they felt safer behind closed doors—or both. It didn't really matter.

On one hand, the blessed calm had been a relief after last night. On the other, the stillness in the house felt ominous somehow. Almost as though it was *too* quiet. She hadn't been able to relax. Instead, Meredith had felt the apprehension building in the pit of her stomach all day, as though her instincts were telling her something bad was about to happen, and every second that passed without it happening just made the waiting so much worse.

It was impossible to forget that there was still a killer in the house. Someone whose identity, whose motives, were still unknown.

Someone who wanted them to be afraid...

She heard the first signs of voices in the dining room. "There they are," Meredith said, shaking off her gloomy thoughts. "I should get this stuff out there."

Picking up the tray, she moved toward the kitchen door. As she pushed through it into the dining room, Meredith kept her fingers crossed that the meal would go smoothly.

They'd already begun gathering, she noted, automatically starting to count all the faces. Her eyes met Tom's, but she didn't let her gaze linger. Giving him a slight nod, she continued with the others. Scott. Rachel. Alex. Greg. And—

"Where's Jess?"

It was Alex who asked the question, voicing exactly what Meredith had been about to think.

She slammed to a stop, her heart seizing at the question. The dishes and silverware clattered on the tray in her hands, the noise jangling her nerves further.

Everyone in the room seemed to freeze, all eyes going to the place where Jessica had sat during the previous meals, including at lunch.

The seat was empty.

"No one's seen her?" Tom asked, glancing at the others.

"No," Greg said. The others shook their heads.

Meredith's gaze flew to Tom's, meeting for a split second before she immediately placed the tray she carried onto the nearest table and moved for the doorway.

"It could be nothing," he said right behind her, and she realized he was following her. From the sound of the footsteps behind her, he wasn't the only one. "She could be fine."

"I hope so," Meredith said. *Prayed it was the case,* was more accurate.

Arriving in the main hall, she hurried up the stairs, doing her best not to break into an all-out run. No need to show how concerned she really was and make everyone more nervous than they had to be.

As soon as she reached the second floor, she saw the door of Jessica's room was closed. Moving straight to it, she knocked on the hard surface, hoping she'd get an angry yell in response. "Jessica?"

No answer. Meredith didn't detect a single sound on the other side of the door.

Her unease growing, she heard those who'd followed her coming to a stop behind her.

"She could be asleep," Rachel suggested weakly, the fear in her voice making it clear how much she believed it.

"Maybe," Scott murmured in a comforting tone, not sounding at all convincing.

"Jessica?" Meredith tried again. When there was still no response, she reached down and tried the knob.

It turned in her hand.

Meredith immediately froze, her fingers holding the knob in midturn as the implications of it sank in. Behind her, someone inhaled sharply, everyone going still.

"She wouldn't have left her door unlocked," Alex said softly, giving voice to what they all were thinking.

No, she certainly wouldn't have. Not as scared and suspicious as Jessica was.

Trying to hold back the terror she felt climbing in her throat, Meredith slowly pushed the door open.

"Jessica?" she called again, just in case, not wanting to surprise the woman if she somehow was fine, somehow hadn't heard the knock. She probably had armed herself, would attack if startled.

The door slowly opened, gradually revealing the room inside. Everything appeared to be quiet and still.

Her heart pounding, deafening in her ears, Meredith took one step into the room, then another.

And stopped.

She didn't need to go any farther. She could see the bed from there.

Could see that Jessica would never answer again.

What stood out the most was the blood. It was splattered across the bedspread, garish and ugly against the muted colors of the comforter.

And in the middle of it was Jessica, lying on top of the mattress, a knife in her chest.

Chapter Twelve

Tom barely had time to process the horrific sight before the first shocked gasp behind him jolted him back to awareness.

"Jess! *No!*" Rachel screamed.

Tom quickly turned around and held out his arms, both to block their view and shepherd them from the room. "All right. Everybody out."

"Are you sure she's dead?" Alex asked hesitantly. "Maybe there's some way…"

From what he'd seen Tom didn't think there was any way Jessica was alive, but this wasn't the time to destroy even the slightest bit of hope for any of them. "I will check to confirm, but in the meantime, everybody needs to go downstairs and wait. Maybe go back to the dining room."

"You can't really expect us to eat at a time like this," Greg objected in disbelief.

"I don't care what you do, but you need to go. This is a crime scene. Unlike with Haley, there's no need to move her, so I'm sure the police would like the room as undisturbed as possible."

"Who put you in charge?" Alex griped.

Tom opened his mouth to respond. Before he could, Meredith did.

"No one," she said behind him. "So I'll say it. Please go downstairs."

At the back of the group, Rick and Ellen needed no encouragement, quickly turning to go.

"It's a good idea," Scott said gently, placing his hands lightly on Rachel's shoulders. "Come on, Rach."

Staring dazedly at Jess, Rachel didn't respond at first. Tears streamed down her cheeks, her mouth hanging open as though in a silent scream. Finally she nodded slightly, allowing him to turn her away from the scene and out of the doorway.

Greg quickly lowered his head and moved away. With one last look into the room, Alex did the same.

Tom closed the door, then turned back toward Meredith. And Jess.

"Thank you," Meredith said softly without looking at him. "I should have thought of that first."

"No problem," he said. "I guess I should check…"

As he moved closer to the body, he could immediately tell without a doubt that Jess was dead. Her eyes were open, staring blankly above, her mouth agape.

He carefully pressed his fingers to the side of her neck, nearly wincing at the sensation. Her skin was already cool to the touch. Still he waited long enough to confirm there was no pulse before pulling his hand away.

Leaning back, he studied her face. She looked terrified, he thought, a lump rising in his throat. She'd known what was happening, known she was dying. If she'd been stabbed in the chest and stomach as it appeared, then she must have faced her killer. Part of him wondered if the horror on her face was from the knowledge of what was happening to her—or from knowing who her killer was.

Reaching out, he gently closed her eyes. Maybe the police wouldn't have wanted him to, something he'd belatedly realized with Haley yesterday, but it didn't seem right leaving her like that, any more than it had with Haley. If the police wanted to make an issue of it, he'd just have to deal with it.

He turned to find Meredith standing with her arms wrapped around herself, still staring at the body. She looked so shattered it was all he could do not to reach out and pull her close.

It seemed to take her a few seconds to realize he was facing her. She finally lifted haunted eyes to meet his. "My God, why is this happening?"

"I don't know," he had to say, no matter how much he hated doing so. "But we're going to figure this out," he continued, needing to hear the words, needing to believe them as much as she did.

She nodded slowly. He couldn't tell if she believed him or was just responding automatically.

"We don't have to move her or touch anything," Meredith murmured. "But we should at least cover her with a sheet. I don't think the police would mind that."

Tom could hear the guilt and anguish that were heavy in her voice, and suspected she was looking for something— anything—she could do for this woman who'd been murdered in her house. It did seem wrong to just walk away and leave her like this for the next several days, as much as it had to leave her with her eyes open. "Sure. Good idea."

"Let me get a fresh sheet." Pulling the door open, she slipped out into the hall.

Leaving him alone with Jess.

She lay in the center of the bed, still dressed in the clothes she'd been wearing earlier. He studied the knife. It looked slightly different from the one used on Haley, but also different from the ones in the house, so likely it was still one the killer had brought here. Evidently the killer didn't have a matched set, he thought darkly, wondering if it meant anything.

In spite of her behavior over the past few days, a wave of guilt washed over him as he remembered some of the things he'd thought of her. No matter how she'd acted or the kind of person she'd been, she didn't deserve this. No one did.

Glancing down, he noticed blood on the floor. There was another trail, the reverse of the one they'd discovered in Haley's room, this time bigger near the door. She must have been stabbed there, then forced back into the room. Had she answered the door to her attacker, or had the killer managed to catch her when she'd been entering the room, maybe on her way back from the bathroom?

A few seconds later, he felt Meredith return. "Got it," she said, holding up the folded sheet she held in one hand.

"Let me help you."

Together they draped the sheet over the body, letting it softly drift over her until she was completely covered.

When it was done, Tom looked at Meredith over the width of the bed. "Should we go downstairs?"

She didn't respond for a moment, studying the covered sheet on the bed. Then she seemed to gather herself, squaring her shoulders, carefully wiping away every trace of vulnerability like a mask falling into place over her face. Meredith Sutton was a tough one, he thought with no small sense of admiration. Maybe that wasn't a surprise given what she'd been through with her ex, although it did make him wonder, not for the first time, why she would have let anyone hurt her.

"Let's go," she said. "I need to make sure everyone else is all right."

WHEN THEY REACHED the bottom of the main staircase, they heard voices coming from the living room. The doors were open. Meredith recognized Alex's and Greg's voices, and figured the others must be in there with them.

Sure enough, the remaining members of the wedding party were clustered together on the couches in the center of the room.

"We thought we'd find you in the dining room," Meredith said.

"Like I said, no one was really in the mood to eat," Greg said. In his right hand, he clutched his flask.

"But you were in the mood to drink?" Rachel sniped.

Greg raised the flask and tipped it toward her. "I'm amazed the rest of you aren't."

"That won't help us get to the bottom of this," Alex said flatly.

"Where are Rick and Ellen?" Meredith asked.

"I think they said they were going back to the kitchen," Rachel said.

Probably not wanting to spend any more time with this group, Meredith thought. Considering everything that had happened, she couldn't blame them.

"I'm still trying to figure out how the killer got to her," Scott said. "We all know how scared Jess was. There's no way she would have left her door unlocked. So how did the killer get to her?"

"She could have opened the door to him, or her, if it was someone she trusted," Alex suggested. As he trailed off, he turned and looked rather pointedly at Rachel.

If she noticed the implication, she didn't show it. "There's another explanation," Rachel said. "Aren't there secret passages in this place? Jess mentioned something about that to me yesterday, something she read about the previous murder here."

She aimed the question directly at Meredith, and there was no missing the accusation in it. Meredith felt every eye in the room turn toward her.

Meredith studied her closely. "Is that what the two of you

were talking about so intently this morning after breakfast when I saw you in the hall?"

Rachel slammed her mouth shut. "No," she said tightly. "She was still mad at me for bringing us here."

"*Are* there secret passages, Meredith?" Greg asked.

"Yes," Meredith admitted. "But they've all been sealed," she quickly added, to stave off the instantaneous panic and outrage she could see rising on their faces. "After what happened before, every single entrance to the passages was closed off. There's no way to access any of them."

"You're sure about that?" Scott said.

"Yes. I oversaw the work myself and checked all of them before you arrived."

"So it's most likely she let the killer in," Alex said.

No one seemed to have an obvious comeback to refute that, the implications lying heavily over the room.

"I don't understand why anybody could be doing this," Scott murmured.

"I'm just going to say it," Alex said sharply. "We should be asking Rachel."

Rachel's eyes flared in alarm. "What are you talking about?"

His face flush with anger, he jabbed a finger in her direction. "You have to know why this is happening. They were *your* friends. *You* brought them here. They wouldn't be dead if it wasn't for you!"

"We don't know that," Rachel insisted, a note of desperate hope in her voice.

"What about Kim? Is it just a coincidence she's dead, too?"

Rachel blinked in shock. "Kim overdosed and drowned in her bathtub at home."

"Yes," Greg said, jumping in. "So now your three closest friends from college are all dead. He's right—it's hard to believe that's a coincidence."

"Kim and I weren't close anymore. We haven't spoken in years."

"So she's the one friend you wouldn't have been able to lure here to be a bridesmaid," Alex noted.

"I did not *lure* anyone here!"

"Didn't you? You're the reason all of us are here. Why did you bring us here?"

"For a wedding! That's all!"

"Why *here?* Why this of all places? Why somewhere that was already connected with murder and death?"

"Because it was so beautiful! A real-life castle, like something out of a fairy tale. That's what I wanted, the fairy-tale wedding! I had no idea any of this would happen!"

"Didn't you?" Alex immediately shot back. "Tell us the truth! Why is this happening?"

Rachel gave her head a desperate shake. "I really don't know!"

For what it was worth, Meredith believed her. The woman's denials rang true, her paleness and anguish in the face of the accusations stark and painful. If she was acting, it was the performance of a lifetime.

Scott took a step in front of her. "Come on, guys," he said, his voice hard. "Back off. She doesn't know anything."

"Are you sure about that?" Alex asked. "You guys were broken up for a long time, and you really haven't been back together all that long. How well do you really know her? Hell, how do you know getting back together wasn't part of some plan on her part?"

"You can't really believe that!" Rachel said.

Alex hesitated, a flicker of uncertainty passing across his face. "I don't know," he admitted. "But all of our lives are on the line here. The questions have to be asked. Nobody else should die because we were all too polite to ask them."

"Well, I don't believe it," Scott said. "And I don't have to ask."

"Then maybe it's a good thing somebody is," Greg mumbled against his flask.

"Where were you this afternoon, Rachel?" Alex asked.

"She was with me," Scott said firmly, a touch of anger climbing into his tone.

"You said the two of you were taking a nap," Alex noted.

"That's right," Scott said.

"So if you were asleep, you have no way of knowing if she was with you in the room the whole time."

The argument seemed to draw Scott up short for a second. An instant later, his expression hardened with certainty. "I *know*."

Alex simply raised his eyebrows, saying nothing, the look answer enough. He was right, Meredith thought. If Scott had been asleep, he couldn't vouch for Rachel's whereabouts the whole time. Of course, the reverse was also true. If Rachel had been asleep, Scott could have slipped out of their room, as well.

"Maybe you do," Alex said, not unkindly. "But there's no way the rest of us can."

"I brought you here to be my friends, not accuse the woman I love of being a killer."

"Well, I didn't come here to die," Alex retorted. "And you might be lovesick enough to trust her after the way she treated you, but the rest of us aren't."

"What are you talking about?" Rachel demanded.

Alex shot a scornful look her way. "Come on, Rach, we all remember what happened in college. The way you dumped him out of nowhere. Or maybe you don't because you weren't around anymore. We're the ones who had to pick up the pieces when he was moping around because you ripped his guts out." He looked at Scott. "When you proposed, I warned you, didn't I? About trusting her again? The warning still stands."

Rachel looked at Scott in shock. "If he didn't approve of you marrying me, why did you ask him to perform the ceremony?"

"He didn't disapprove, he just raised the issue. It's what he does, he asks questions. And you wanted us to get married in the middle of nowhere! I didn't want someone we didn't even know doing it, so it made the most sense."

"That doesn't make sense at all," Rachel snapped.

"Everyone calm down," Tom said. "This isn't getting us anywhere."

"Isn't it?" Alex asked. "What do you suggest, Tom? We need to figure out who's doing this before someone else gets hurt."

"I agree," Tom said. "But turning on each other and blindly throwing around a bunch of accusations isn't going to get us anywhere."

"Look where it got Jess," Greg mused darkly.

Everyone looked at him in horror. "Will you *shut up!*" Rachel screamed at him.

He eyed her coolly. "Or what? You have a knife handy?"

The response seemed to shock everyone into silence. Rachel's jaw moved up and down, but no sound came out. Finally, she clamped her lips together and turned away from him with barely concealed fury. "I knew we shouldn't have invited *you.*"

Greg frowned in mock outrage. "Hey, he's the one giving you the inquisition, and *I'm* the one you regret inviting? What kind of sense does that make?"

"Fine," Rachel spat. "I regret inviting both of you."

"I think it's safe to say we regret that you did, too," Greg returned.

"Greg, please," Scott said with thinly concealed impatience. "This isn't helping."

Greg shrugged. "I wasn't trying to."

Meredith had already been growing tired of the man's antics, and she'd finally reached the end of her tolerance. "Why not?" she challenged. "Don't you want to figure out who's responsible for this?"

"Sure, but it looks like Alex has that covered."

"You seem awfully calm given the circumstances," Meredith noted.

He raised his flask. "A little liquid courage goes a long way."

Fully out of patience, she automatically reached out and grabbed the flask from him. His reflexes likely impaired, he moved too slowly to retain his hold on it, his fingers closing around empty air a moment later.

His eyes narrowed, glittering with suppressed fury. He slowly held out his hand. "I'm going to ask you to give that back," he said with deadly calm.

"I think you've had enough courage for now. It would be helpful if you did without for a while."

"You know you have a house full of alcohol. Taking one little flask isn't going to stop me from getting a drink if I want one."

"Well, this is one less drink for you to have, and right now that sounds good to me."

He glared up at her, the look in his stare sending a shiver of warning through her. Then he pointedly looked away. "Suit yourself."

"Good," Meredith said. Shoving the flask into her pants pocket, she glanced around the room. "Now I still need to check on Rick and Ellen and try the phone lines again. Can everyone please stay calm while I do that?"

It took a few moments, but she eventually received a few nods in response.

"Thank you," she said, meaning it. "I'll be right back."

Meredith quickly turned and stepped out into the hall. She felt Tom fall into line beside her. She didn't question his impulse to come with her. Given the current situation and how tense things that gotten, it felt good not to be alone.

They'd crossed the main hall and were entering the side corridor leading to the kitchen, safely out of earshot of everyone in the living room, when she finally spoke. "We have to figure out who's behind this. If we don't, the killer might not have to bother taking anyone else out. They'll all kill each other."

"This might be what the killer wants," Tom noted gravely. "Haley's body was left out to be found and create fear. Even if Jess's wasn't, that still might be what he or she wants. To keep everybody on edge and turning on one another."

His words sent a tremor of unease rumbling through her. "But why?" she asked automatically, even though she knew he didn't have the answer. It was more a groan of frustration than an actual question.

As expected, he didn't respond, the tension and frustration emanating from him palpable in the close confines of the hallway.

Two people were dead, and they still were no closer to understanding why.

Chapter Thirteen

They found Rick and Ellen in the kitchen. The pair looked up warily at their entrance, Rick from his seat at the island, Ellen from where she stood at the counter.

"Are you both okay?" Meredith asked.

"As well as we can be," Ellen said. "Compared to what I saw upstairs, I can't complain."

Spotting the phone on the wall, Meredith moved toward it.

"It's still not working," Rick said just as Meredith pulled the phone from the wall and raised it to her ear. "Checked it a few minutes ago."

The silence that met her ear confirmed the statement. "Of course," Meredith said as she replaced the receiver. "I should have known you would."

"Can't hurt to keep checking," Ellen murmured.

"Did either of you see anything today?" Tom asked. "Anyone coming out of Jessica's room? Anyone looking suspicious?"

"Nope," Rick said.

"Like I told Meredith," Ellen said. "I hadn't seen anybody in hours before dinner."

They sounded honest enough. "Everybody's in the living room if you want to join us," Meredith offered. It might be better if they all stuck together. She'd certainly feel better if she knew where each person was. Still, she would understand if they turned down the offer, wanting to be nowhere near the people who kept getting murdered, one of whom—if Rick and Ellen weren't involved—was likely the killer.

"Think I'm going to tuck in early," Rick said flatly. "So I can get started digging my way to the garage in the morning."

"Me, too," Ellen said. "Just as soon as I get this food put away."

Meredith looked at the meal Ellen had prepared, all of it untouched. Ellen had the storage containers, aluminum foil and plastic wrap out. Meredith figured if anyone was hungry later, it would at least be in the refrigerator. "That's fine."

"I can help you dig tomorrow if you have more than one shovel," Tom told Rick.

The other man eyed him gravely, as though considering whether he trusted him. After a moment, he nodded slowly. "That'd be a big help."

"Great," Meredith said. "I'll see you both in the morning then."

She quickly turned toward the door, Tom moving to follow. The whole way there, she felt their eyes on her.

No doubt ruing the day they'd ever agreed to work here.

THE MEMBERS OF the wedding party were still in the living room where they'd left them. Everyone was sitting apart from each other, and no one was speaking. Even Scott and Rachel sat on different sides of the room, with Rachel's back rather pointedly to him.

Greg had a glass of amber-colored liquid in his hand, Meredith couldn't help noticing. Evidently he'd found the bar. He'd been right, she thought, feeling the weight of his flask in her pocket. Her victory had been a hollow one.

They all looked up when Tom and Meredith entered.

"Any luck with the phones?" Scott asked.

"No," Meredith said. "They're still out."

No one seemed surprised, or even disappointed. She understood their reaction—or lack of it. It probably had seemed too much to hope for that the phones would be back up right when they were needed more than ever.

Meredith had expected the group to be in a hurry to get back to the safety of their rooms, but no one made a move to leave. Rachel still seemed miffed with Scott, so Meredith could understand why they might not feel like being alone together. Greg likely didn't want to leave the bar. Alex might want to remain where he could question people.

Then again, Jess's death seemed to indicate they weren't safe in their rooms, either. Staying together might seem much more reassuring at the moment.

She surveyed Scott and Rachel sitting at opposite sides of the room. They'd been nearly inseparable since they'd gotten here, making it impossible to speak with either of them alone.

This might be a rare chance to talk to them separately. She had to take advantage of it.

Meredith leaned toward Tom. "I'd like to try to talk to Rachel," she whispered. "See if I can get her to open up."

He gave a slight nod. "I'll talk to Scott. I haven't really had a chance to since all of this started."

"Good idea."

Moving away, she casually made her way over to where Rachel sat. Her heart twisted at the sight of the other woman. She sat with her head bent, her hands clutched tightly in from of her.

"Hey," Meredith said, easing herself into the chair next to Rachel's. "How are you doing?" As soon as she heard the question, she nearly cringed. It was a question she'd come to hate over the past few years. She'd been asked it herself numerous times. She knew it was typically motivated by genuine concern, or was simply a polite way to start a conversation. But usually when it was asked, it was perfectly clear how the person was doing. Just like it was now. With everything that was happening, Rachel couldn't be doing particularly well.

If Rachel thought the question was inane, she didn't show it. She slowly shook her head. "I don't know. I don't understand what's happening, or *why* it's happening, or any of this…. None of it seems real. I keep thinking I'm going to wake up and it'll all turn out to be some terrible nightmare, like I'm dreaming about the worst possible thing that could ever happen at my wedding." She released a short, humorless laugh. "I thought the worst that could happen would be if something happened to my dress or we got stranded at the airport, but this…"

"I don't think anyone could have imagined this," Meredith said.

"But still, Alex is right, just like Jess—" she swallowed hard at her friend's name "—Jess was this morning. This is my fault. I brought us here."

"The only person at fault is the killer."

"Even if that's true, if we get out of here, I've only given them more reason to hate me."

"I'm sure they don't hate you," Meredith said. Remembering Alex's reaction, she wasn't sure it was true, but it seemed like the only thing she could say.

"I didn't realize they were angry at me for breaking up with Scott in college. Maybe I should have, but all that mattered was that Scott and I were back together and the love we felt for each other was still there." She swallowed hard, her voice softening. "This morning Jess told me that maybe I should have taken what happened in college as a sign that Scott and I aren't meant to be together. What if she was right?"

"What did happen between the two of you in college? If you don't mind my asking."

Rachel's expression went blank. She didn't say anything for a long moment, her gaze faraway. Finally she lowered her eyes, giving her head a small shake. "It doesn't matter. It was a long time ago. It's in the past."

I'm not so sure about that, Meredith thought. Given everything that was happening to members of her college group, it seemed more likely than not that something from the past wasn't staying there. She studied the woman's face, more convinced than ever Rachel was hiding something. Whether it was because she truly didn't believe it was relevant or because she didn't think it was any of Meredith's business, it made no difference.

Either way, Rachel wasn't talking.

As soon as Tom saw Meredith sit beside Rachel, he turned and moved to where Scott sat across the room. Scott leaned back in an overstuffed leather chair, his gaze distant as he stared straight in front of him.

Tom lowered himself into the chair beside him. "Hey, Scotty. You doing okay?"

Scott let out a long, slow breath. "Honestly? I don't know." He turned and looked at Tom, mustering a weak smile. "I'm glad you're here, man. With Alex throwing accusations around and Greg drinking everything he can get his hands on, it's good to have somebody I can count on around here."

Tom glanced over to where Greg sat in an isolated corner. He held a glass in one hand, though he wasn't drinking from it. Instead, he stared at the liquid it contained, seemingly lost in thought. "He didn't waste any time finding the bar, did he?"

"No," Scott said with a grimace. "The sad thing is, he told me last year that he stopped drinking, but I guess that didn't last. It's one thing I told Rachel to talk her into inviting him. With Alex performing the ceremony and it looking like you weren't going to make it, I needed someone to be my best man. I mean, there are a couple of guys I work with I could have asked, but it would have felt strange having somebody here who wasn't part of the group, you know? I would have felt bad asking them to come all this way to spend a weekend with a bunch of people they didn't know." Scott sighed. "Now I guess it's a good thing I didn't invite anyone else. I would have hated to put anyone else through this."

"Did Alex really try to talk you out of marrying Rachel?"

"It wasn't like that. It was like he said. He asked me if I really believed I could trust her after how she treated me in college. I figured a minister would do the same thing, right? Make sure you really want to marry somebody? I told him we were both more mature now. Seven years is a long time."

"You never did tell me. Why'd she break up with you?"

Scott sighed. "Guess there's no reason not to tell you. You remember how crazy things were senior year. Between work and juggling classes I was barely keeping my head above water. She thought I was neglecting her, not paying her enough attention. The fact is, she was right. With everything else, I didn't have much time for her. She knew I loved her. At least I thought she did. But I guess it wasn't enough."

He shook his head. "I was doing it for us. So we could have a good life. That's the whole reason I was working so hard. To give her the life she deserved. What I didn't know was that she didn't want somebody who'd have to work so hard for it. She wanted somebody who could afford to take care of her. Somebody with money."

For the first time, Tom heard the hint of bitterness in his old friend's words. They may have gotten past it, but it seemed Scott hadn't completely forgotten how she'd treated him—or how it had felt.

"She told you that?" Tom asked, more than a little stunned.

"No. She just left it at the neglecting-her part. She cut off all contact, refusing to talk to me, refusing to see me. Her friends were all the same way. Jess, Haley, Kim. They all acted like I suddenly didn't exist anymore." A hard look flashed across his face, the expression so fleeting Tom almost missed it.

"It was Kim who told me the truth. I went to their apartment to try to get Rachel to talk to me, to tell her that I'd learned my lesson and wouldn't take her for granted anymore. Kim refused to let me see her, and when I wouldn't go away, she finally came out with it." He drew in a breath. "She said Rachel had decided she couldn't waste any more time with me. She wanted someone with the 'resources' to give her the life she wanted, and that wasn't me."

Even after all these years, the pain was evident in Scott's voice as he related it. Tom wasn't surprised. He knew how much Scott had to have been wounded by that. Scott hadn't come from money, but he'd been smart and a hard worker, using scholarship money to pay for school. Meanwhile, Rachel's family had been well-off. It had been a sore point for Scott. To have that be the reason she'd broken up with him… No wonder he hadn't wanted to talk about it.

Kim would have known what hearing that would have been like for Scott, too. Yet she'd told him anyway. Tom didn't know if it was kinder for him to know the truth, or if she'd simply been cruel by telling him. "Is that what Jess meant when she implied Kim wouldn't have been invited even if she were alive?" he asked. "Because she'd told you that?"

"No, Kim had a falling-out with the rest of them a few years ago. Jess is actually the one who told me about it, since Rachel and I weren't together then. Evidently Kim's drinking had gotten worse after college, and she'd developed a drug habit, as well. She showed up high at some event Haley was holding and made a scene. Apparently they'd been trying to help her before then, but after that, they washed their hands of her. It sounds like she got clean last year and tried getting in touch with them, maybe to make amends, but whatever it was she'd done, they weren't interested."

"And now she's dead, too," Tom said softly, wondering if Alex was right and there was a connection. They'd said she'd overdosed and drowned in her bathtub—an accident, not a violent murder—but was it possible there was more to it than that?

"And Rachel's the only one left," Scott said, glancing over at his fiancée.

Tom followed his gaze, watching the woman talk with Meredith. Now that he knew what had happened between her and Scott all those years ago, he couldn't help but view her with fresh eyes. "I have to say, I'm kind of surprised you'd want to have anything to do with Rachel after she treated you like that, let alone marry her."

"Maybe there was a part of me that agreed with her," Scott said quietly. "That didn't think I was good enough for her. And now I am." Something in his voice sent an uncomfortable feeling down Tom's spine, a certain hardness that matched the stoniness of his expression as he stared at Rachel.

"And we both know it."

By NINE O'CLOCK, everyone was ready to retreat to their rooms. They wasted no time doing so, Greg and Alex heading straight up without a look back. Even Scott and Rachel, without a word and only the barest glance between them, moved silently upstairs.

And Meredith and Tom were alone again.

They sat together on one of the couches in the middle of the room. Meredith leaned back in her seat, puzzling over the multitude of questions running through her head.

"So Rachel broke up with Scott in college because he didn't have any money," Meredith mused. "I can't believe he'd want to get back together with her after that."

"That's what I told him," Tom said. "But the more I think about it, it makes a kind of sad sense. Rachel's family was loaded and she inherited a lot of money when her father died. Scott was in school on scholarships and I know he always kind of felt he wasn't good enough for her. It had to have killed him to hear that was why she'd dumped him. But now he's made it, and he's proven to her—and himself—that he is good enough." He shook his head. "I knew it must have meant a lot to him to be able to give her a wedding in a place like this. I just wish he knew he didn't have to prove himself like that to anybody, himself included."

Meredith turned the information over in her mind. She knew he wouldn't like what she had to say, but she had to say it. "Do you think he might have had an ulterior motive to bring her—to bring all of you—here?"

It took a second, but Tom jerked his head toward her, and Meredith knew he'd picked up on her implication. "You think *Scott* killed Haley and Jess? Why?"

"Maybe revenge?" she suggested carefully. "She dumped him, all her friends turned their backs on him. This could be some sick way of getting back at them, and punishing Rachel."

"That's way too twisted, and not something Scott is remotely capable of. He's not a killer."

She hated the pain she heard in his voice and wished she could let it go, but she couldn't. "He could have changed over the years without you noticing it. You said you didn't keep in touch much, only met or talked a few times a year when you were in Chicago."

Meredith watched his jaw tighten with anger. "Scott's not a killer." His tone allowed for no further argument. "What about Rachel? Alex is right, she's the one who brought everyone here. And she decided to get back together with Scott after all this time, too."

Meredith thought back to her conversation with the woman, remembering the genuine sadness she'd heard in her voice. At least she'd thought it was genuine. At this point, who knew what to believe? "What's her motive?"

Tom was silent for a long moment, finally letting out a long breath. "I don't know. There's still so much going on here we don't know about."

"And we're figuring it out too slowly." And two people were dead, and more lives were in jeopardy as long as they continued fumbling around in the dark.

A wave of frustration and despair washed over her. Overwhelmed by the feeling, Meredith gave her head a small shake.

Tom didn't fail to notice. "What is it?" he asked.

"Part of me can't help wishing Adam was here," she admitted. "He would know what to do. No hesitation, no doubt. Just action."

"You and your brother must be close," he said.

She nodded. "We were all we had growing up. Our parents weren't what anyone would call loving. Our father only cared about his career and making money, and our mother didn't have a maternal bone in her body. I always had the feeling they only had children because it was what they were supposed to do, and they would have been perfectly happy without us. Adam was five when I was born, and he looked out for me, up until the time he left for college."

"It sounds like it's a good thing you had each other."

"It was." She smiled sadly. "The funny thing is, I used to resent him a little, too. Our mother wasn't exactly nurturing, but Adam was still her golden child. He was handsome and brilliant, while I was awkward and quiet. He was the valedictorian of his class in high school. I was the salutatorian of mine." Story of her life. Never quite good enough. Always second best.

"That's still impressive."

"Not really. You know what they say. 'Second place is the first loser.'"

He frowned. "Who says that?"

She grimaced at the memory. "My mother did, actually."

"No offense, but she doesn't sound like somebody who's worth listening to."

"I know that now," she conceded. "Unfortunately some things aren't that easy to shake. Growing up, it seemed like no matter what I did, all I ever heard was 'That's not what Adam would have done!' And for the past few days in the back of my head, I keep hearing, 'That's not what Adam would do!'" *Or would he have had to do any of this?* she wondered. Would he have realized what was happening before it did, stopping the murder before it ever happened? Would he have somehow known who the killer was and recognized what they had planned?

There was no way of knowing. Adam wasn't here. She was. And she was responsible for everything that happened here—and the lives of everyone at Sutton Hall.

"You're doing great," Tom said firmly. "No one could question the choices you've made. You've done the best you could under the circumstances. We're going to get through this."

She looked up into his strong, solemn face. She wasn't entirely certain she believed him, but at the moment, she was grateful for the kindness.

"What about you?" she asked. "Do you have any brothers or sisters?"

"One of each," he said with a smile. "They're great."

If they were anything like him, she believed it. Because he was great. Strong and loyal and brave, and smart and considerate and caring. Again there was that sense of amazement in the back of her mind that someone so good-looking could be even better on the inside, as great as this man was.

It suddenly struck her just how much she liked him. She simply *liked* him, as a person, who he was deep down. She couldn't remember the last time she'd met someone she simply liked on a basic, instinctive level. Maybe she never had. She'd certainly never met anyone like him before. If only she had. If only he'd noticed her. If only she'd been brave enough back then…

It was foolish to think that way. There was no changing the past, no way to go back. Thinking about it was a waste of time. All that mattered was that she *had* met him— here, now—at a time, at a moment when she needed him. It was the lone bright spot in these terrible few days, and she would always be grateful he'd been here for her, even as she couldn't help wishing he hadn't had to be.

Suddenly realizing just how long she'd been sitting there staring into his eyes, she made herself look away, even as part of her regretted breaking the unexpected intimacy they shared.

Even as part of her recognized that as long as she'd been staring into his eyes, he'd been staring back.

"We should get to bed," Meredith said. "You're going

to need the rest if you're going to work with Rick in the morning."

Tom frowned. "What about you? What are you going to do?"

"I'll watch over everyone else, try keep an eye on them and make sure nothing happens."

"And who'll keep an eye out for you?"

It was a valid question, and she couldn't help feel a flicker of apprehension as she thought about it. She did her best to shake it off, the way she had to. "I'll just have to keep an eye out for myself. I am the one in charge here, right?"

He didn't respond, but she didn't miss the way his lips thinned with disapproval. She knew what he was thinking, but she meant what she said.

As much as she appreciated him being here for her, when it came right down to it, the only one a person could rely on was her—or him—self. She'd learned that the hard way with Brad, when she'd failed to be strong enough, failed to defend herself. She couldn't do that again, couldn't be that weak. She was going to have to take care of herself.

Learning how to do that was a long time in the making.

Two down...

Poor, stupid Jess. So scared. So cautious. And in the end, she hadn't seen it coming.

She'd left her room to use the bathroom, and on her way back she'd let her guard down at just exactly the wrong moment. She'd been a step away from being safely back in her room.

Instead, she'd met her fate.

A memory of the way her face had looked at that moment lingered. No, she hadn't seen it coming—the first stab at least.

The second and the third...those she'd seen.

And in the final moments, when she'd been told exactly why she'd had to die, a flash of recognition had passed over her eyes, briefly eclipsing the fear.

In the end, though, the fear had won out. The sheer terror that she was about to die.

And then she had.

The fear was the most satisfying part. Dying wasn't enough. They deserved to suffer.

One of them in particular… That would happen soon enough.

Everything was going according to plan. Soon it would be over.

And justice would be served at last.

Chapter Fourteen

Tom was up early the next morning. He'd had too much running through his head to let him get much sleep. Too many vivid memories of Haley and Jess, as they'd looked in life—and death. Too many questions and too few answers. Too many doubts about the people around him, both the strangers and his old friends.

Too many thoughts of Meredith, peering up at him, vulnerable and lovely and brave.

Meredith, looking terrified as the murderer moved in on her for the kill—

It was the last thought that finally forced him out of bed. He would sleep when this was over, when they were safe.

A check out his window confirmed that the snow seemed to have slowed down. The flurries weren't coming down nearly as hard or fast as they had been the past two days. Unfortunately, he still got no signal on his phone. Pulling on his boots and warmest clothes, Tom took his coat with him when he left his room. He wasn't sure when Rick would want to get started on digging out to the garage, but he wanted to be prepared. The sooner they got the process started, the better.

There was no answer at Meredith's door when he knocked. Fighting the nervousness clawing up his spine, he told himself she must have gotten up already and gone downstairs. A burst of anger rose from the pit of his stomach at the idea of her wandering around alone, even though he had no right to tell her what to do. This was her house. That didn't mean he had to like it. Frustration burned in his gut.

The only person in the kitchen when he walked in was Ellen. She looked up from the counter at his entrance, a distinct wariness in her eyes as they flew toward the door.

Doing his best to squelch his disappointment at finding her alone, Tom forced a smile he wasn't close to feeling, hoping to put the woman at ease. "Good morning."

She managed to return the gesture with a small, polite smile of her own before quickly lowering her eyes to the counter. "Morning."

"Have you seen Meredith?"

"She and Rick went to get some supplies they thought you both might need to get to the garage."

His first instinct was to ask where exactly they'd gone, so he could go there, so he could see her. Swallowing the words, Tom drew in a slow breath. Meredith was fine. He'd see her soon enough.

He slowly realized that, in the meantime, this was the first opportunity he'd had to be alone with the cook. The woman remained a mystery to him, probably more so than anyone in this place. And if he was inclined to believe Rick wasn't the killer, that meant Ellen was the most likely option.

She started to turn toward the stove. Tom didn't miss the fact that she didn't put her back to him entirely as she worked, keeping him in front of her the whole time. Because she didn't trust him, or because she was pretending not to?

"So, Ellen," he said, doing his best to sound casual. "How long have you been a cook?"

He saw an unexpected spark of amusement enter her eyes. "You sure you're not a reporter, too?"

He had to grin at that. "I'm sure."

Her lips quirking, she shook her head. "All my life, really. But only a few years now as a job."

"What'd your family think about you taking a job here? They must be worried that they haven't heard from you in a while."

The look she shot him said she knew full well he was fishing. Still she answered. "I don't have any. Not anymore," she added after a beat.

"I'm sorry."

Ellen shrugged. "I'm not. Sometimes you're better off. I used to have a husband, until he found a pretty young thing he liked better and took off. It was a lousy thing to do, but I know I'm better off without him."

He eyed her carefully. "I wouldn't blame you if you're pretty cynical about marriage after that. You didn't have any doubts about working here and cooking for weddings?"

"A job's a job. And I'm not that cynical. Certainly not cynical enough to start killing bridesmaids, if that's what you're implying."

Okay, so he'd been grasping at straws. Damn, he needed some answers.

Ellen shook her head. "I've had enough tough times in my life to learn that all you can do is pick yourself up and move on." She paused just long enough to send him one more, rather pointed look. "You'd be surprised how much a woman can overcome. Especially if she has the right person to help her."

The words seemed loaded with meaning, and Tom wasn't sure at first how to interpret them. Who had she had to help her? And what was her purpose in telling him…

Then in a flash he understood.

She wasn't talking about herself. She was talking about Meredith.

And him.

He suddenly remembered the way she'd looked at him and Meredith yesterday, that gleam in her eye. Was she simply imagining things, or had she sensed something between them?

He had to admit, if she had sensed something, she wasn't imagining it. There was something between him and Meredith, a connection he never would have expected, especially not now, not under these circumstances, when there were so many more important things to think about, when people were dying and lives were on the line.

Or maybe that was exactly the time to see things, feel things, so much more clearly. They were surrounded by so much uncertainty, there was little time to waste questioning feelings or wondering about emotions. They were fighting for survival, relying on their guts and instincts to get them through.

And every instinct he had was pointing him toward Meredith.

The door suddenly swung open. A moment later Meredith stepped through.

At the sight of her, his lungs relaxed slightly, easing a tension he hadn't realized he'd still been holding in his chest. She looked over at him and smiled.

Damned if something didn't clutch in his chest all over again.

"Good morning," she said.

"Morning."

"You ready?" Rick asked, having followed Meredith into the room. The handyman was obviously prepared to go, his gloves and hat already in place.

"Absolutely," Tom said.

"You haven't had anything to eat yet," Ellen protested.

Tom reached out and plucked a muffin from the plate

she'd just placed on the countertop. "Done." He turned to Rick. "Let's do this."

The sooner they got to work, the sooner they would be out of here, be safe.

He looked at Meredith, the urgency building in his gut. All of them.

"I WONDER HOW it's going out there," Meredith murmured. She peered through the window above the kitchen sink at the world beyond. Not that what she was looking for would be visible outside the window anyway.

The snow hadn't stopped entirely, but had thankfully tapered off enough that she could at least get a glimpse of the outside world through the flurries, even if most of what she could see was several towering feet of snow. Opening the front doors of Sutton Hall, Meredith had found the snowfall came up to her chest.

It had been hours since Tom and Rick had left, armed with two shovels and a plan to hollow out a path from the house to the garage. They hadn't come back, hadn't been heard from since.

"I'm sure we'll hear soon enough," Ellen said, rinsing off the dishes in the sink to prepare them for the dishwasher. "They'll be wanting lunch pretty soon."

Meredith would have thought they would have wanted it long ago. Lunchtime had passed over an hour ago. The rest of the wedding party had come and gone already.

She did her best to fight the anxiety churning in her belly. They were probably fine. They were busy, of course. The task they'd gone to accomplish wasn't an easy one. It would take them several hours at least to make it to the garage. Or maybe they'd made it there and had started working on the plow, getting so caught up in it they'd forgotten about lunch.

Maybe…

"I should have gone with them," Meredith said, mostly to herself. "It's my job. I should have offered to help, too."

"Only two shovels," Ellen pointed out.

Meredith couldn't argue with that. It didn't make her feel better. At least if she was out there she would know if they were okay.

If Tom was okay...

She nearly shook herself. She knew she was being ridiculous. She had no reason to think anything had happened to them. Not that she thought Rick would do anything to Tom, even if he was the killer. It would be too obvious he was responsible.

Unless it looked like an accident...

Or the killer came up behind them unnoticed while they were busy working, striking before they could do anything about it—

Jerking upright, Meredith pushed away from the counter. "I'm going to go see if there's any sign of them."

One corner of her mouth twitching, Ellen sent her an all-too-knowing look before turning back to the dishes with a shrug. "Suit yourself."

Meredith was already stepping away from the sink, heading for the door. Suddenly she stopped, reconsidering. Wandering through the house on her own still seemed like a risky idea. Spotting a rolling pin lying on the countertop nearby, she grabbed it, relishing the weight of it in her hand.

She hurried through the dining room, keeping a close eye on her surroundings. The garage was on the west side of the property, on the other side of the house. To find the shortest route there possible, Tom and Rick had left through a door in the back of the west wing. She'd have to use the same one.

Crossing through the main foyer, she made her way to the corridor running the length of the west wing. They weren't using this side of the house as much, she reflected, taking in the row of closed doors. The east wing had been in better shape and less in need of restoration when they'd come here, so it had only made sense to start there. Not to mention the kitchen and dining room were there. They were finally almost done with the restorations over here. They just hadn't decided what to do with these rooms yet.

If they would need to do anything with them, Meredith reflected. After this weekend, they weren't likely to have any guests, so the rooms would likely—

She heard them a split second too late, the footsteps rushing up behind her. She automatically started to turn—

She never had the chance. Something hard and solid hit her upper back.

She flew forward, knocked straight off her feet. The rolling pin burst out of her hand before she could think to grab it tighter. The ground came rushing up at her. She barely had time to throw her arms out before she crashed into the ground.

She didn't have time to recover, didn't have time to move. Suddenly a hand fisted in her hair, yanking hard. Before she could cry out from the pain, from the fear, her head was slammed down into the floor. Every bone in her skull seemed to crash together. Stars exploded before her eyes, blurring her vision.

Dazed, she barely registered something tugging at her hip. No, her pocket…

She understood in a flash. Her keys. They were going for her keys.

Fighting the cloud of pain fogging her brain, she lashed out, kicking her legs, thrashing from side to side. Sucking in a breath, she threw her mouth open and yelled as loud as she could.

Even to her ears it sounded weak, a low moan instead of the scream she wanted—needed—to release.

Panicked, terrified, determined to fight them off, it took her a moment to realize the hands were no longer at her side. She couldn't feel anyone's presence nearby.

They were gone.

"Meredith?"

The voice came from farther down the hall ahead of her. *Tom,* she recognized, relief flooding through her.

"Meredith!"

Moments later she felt a hand on her shoulder. She instinctively flinched, until the gentleness of the touch registered.

"Hey," he said, his voice again a balm on her nerves.

She slowly rolled onto her side, trying to ignore the throbbing in her head. She placed her hand on the floor to push herself up to an upright position.

"Easy," he said, reaching out to help her sit up. She looked up to find him kneeling beside her. "What happened?"

"Someone knocked me down," she said, wincing at both the pain and the memory. "They hit me, slammed my head into the floor..." She swallowed, the memories rushing back.

It was all painfully familiar. The feeling of being pushed, of being struck, of someone on top of her, of her head being knocked into the floor—

The back of her eyes began to burn. She immediately closed them and lowered her head, refusing to let the tears come, to give into the emotion, to let Tom see.

He swore. "You could have been killed."

Every instinct she had automatically rejected the idea. "No," she said faintly. She thought back to what had happened. "I don't think they were trying to kill me. I felt them fumbling for my pockets. They were trying to take my keys."

"And they damn well could have killed you to get them."

His voice was tight with anger, though not toward her, she knew. She was familiar with that sound.

She felt a finger touch lightly under her chin, prompting her to raise her head. She didn't resist. The finger disappeared. Then, so softly she didn't realize it at first, his hands were sliding against her cheeks, cradling her face.

"Look at me," he ordered, the tone soft but firm. She raised her eyes to obey.

And found herself looking straight into his.

The breath caught in her throat. She peered, helplessly, into his eyes, into his face, until everything else in the world seemed to fade away. There was nothing but the man in front of her, looking back at her. The tightness that had been gripping her body gradually eased, her racing heartbeat slowing to a steady, even throb.

He really did have the bluest eyes she'd ever seen. It seemed as though she could get lost in them forever, drifting in a sea of deep, bottomless blue. Yet it was more than the color than pulled her in. It was the kindness she saw in them, the empathy, the humanity. In the back of her mind she recognized that she'd never seen such a look in Brad's eyes. Not for her, not for anything. Because he hadn't been a good man. And Tom Campbell was, deep in his core. She felt the unmistakable truth of it in hers.

The warmth of his hands on her cheeks, the softness of his skin, slowly sank into her system. The thumb of his right hand gently stroked over her skin. His gaze slowly lowered, drifting down her face. She finally realized where that thumb was placed, just above her upper lip. He focused there for an infinite moment, and she suddenly had the feeling that he was about to kiss her.

But he didn't. The corner of his mouth quirking with

what seemed like a trace of regret, he had raised his eyes to hers but moved no closer.

"Are you okay?" he asked, the low timbre of his voice seeming to vibrate right through her.

She managed a small nod. "I think so."

"I shouldn't have left you alone."

As much as part of her couldn't help but respond to hearing that sentiment from this man, it still grated. Meredith slowly leaned back, pulling out of his grasp, forcing him to let her go. "You're not responsible for me. And I don't need a babysitter."

"I didn't say you did," he said. "But given everything that's happened, we should have realized it wasn't safe for anyone to be alone in this place.

"We had no reason to believe I was in danger. This all seemed to be centered around you and your friends."

"There's a killer on the loose. *Everyone* is in danger."

At the moment she could hardly argue with that. "Why would somebody want my keys?"

He appeared to consider the question, his eyebrows drawing together. "Only two reasons I can think of. They're afraid of someone else getting access to their room and want to get the keys before someone else can—"

"Or they're the one who wants access to someone else's room," Meredith finished.

Tom nodded gravely. "And if that's the case, that most likely means the killer has another intended victim."

It certainly made the most sense. After what happened to Jessica, everyone was going to be far more cautious. The killer's only chance of getting to another victim might be to break into their room.

She automatically placed her hand over her pocket, feeling the reassuring shape of the keys through the fabric. "At least they didn't get them," she murmured. "Unfortunately,

I don't think this is going to stop them from trying another way to get to whoever they want."

"Or from trying to come after you again," he suggested, his voice tight with anger. "Let's go find out where everyone is right now. Maybe we can narrow down who could have done this. It might give us an idea who's behind the murders."

"All right," she said, starting to push to her feet.

Tom immediately rose to his, bending to offer his hand to help her up.

She hesitated for a slightest instant, then slowly slid her hand onto his. The warmth of his skin sent a charge straight through her. She did her best to keep the reaction from showing on her face, even as her whole body seemed to buzz from the effects of it. Once she was on her feet, she quickly pulled her fingers from his. "Thanks."

He let her lead the way to the front hall, following so close behind she could feel him there. By the time they reached the staircase, she was feeling better. Stronger.

Angrier.

She plunged up the stairs, ready to get some answers.

They were halfway up when a muffled cry of pain cut through the air.

They both froze for a split second. Meredith's gut clenched painfully. *Oh, God. No.*

She took off in an instant, bursting up the remaining steps, Tom right by her side. Finally arriving at the second floor, she skidded to a stop, taking in the scene before them.

No!

The word was screaming in her mind, but Meredith couldn't utter a sound.

Greg lay facedown in the hallway, the back of his head coated in blood.

Chapter Fifteen

Greg?"

Meredith took off down the hallway, Tom right at her side, her heart lodged in her throat at the sight of the big, unmoving form lying on the floor.

A split second before they reached him, he shifted slightly, the sight sending fresh shock ripping through her. At the sight of him, she'd immediately thought he had to be dead. The fact that he wasn't was almost as much of a shock as finding him there.

He rolled partway on his side, then flopped back onto his stomach, placing a hand on the floor to steady himself.

"Take it easy," Tom said, dropping to his knee at Greg's side. "You're hurt."

"Am I?" Greg asked, sounding bemused.

"What happened?" Meredith asked.

Greg pushed himself fully onto one side, peering up at Meredith, his eyes narrowed in pain. "Guess I should have listened to you and cut back on the drinks. I must have tripped."

"You tripped and hit yourself in the back of the head?" Tom asked in disbelief.

Greg chuckled weakly. "It happens. Believe me."

"That's not what happened here," Meredith said, looking beyond him. She stepped past him and picked up something from the floor a few feet away. It was a candlestick one that normally sat on the hallway table a short distance from here. The base was smeared with blood. "Someone hit you," she said, holding up the candlestick. "With this

Greg glared blearily at the offending object. "I guess should be glad it wasn't a knife."

"What's going on?"

The voice came from the end of the hall near the stair Meredith jerked her head up to find Scott standing there, bottle of water in one hand, staring at them.

As though cued by his voice, the door to the bridal suit opened. Rachel tentatively stepped into the hallway. Sh came to an abrupt stop when she saw them. "What hap pened?"

"Someone hit Greg in the back of the head," Meredit said.

"Who?" Rachel asked.

"We don't know," Tom said with strained patience. "D you hear anything?"

"I went down to the kitchen to get Rachel some water Scott said, holding up the bottle he held.

Rachel shook her head. "I didn't hear anything."

Greg started to push up on his elbows to hoist himse from the floor. "This is all very interesting, but I think I like to go back to my room."

"Maybe you shouldn't move," Tom suggested.

"I'm not going to lie here in the middle of the hall Greg grumbled. "That didn't work out so well for Hale now did it?"

There didn't seem to be any arguing with him. Rath than let him fall over, Tom reached for Greg's arm an steadied him as he rose to his feet.

"I'll get a first-aid kit," Meredith said.

"I'll get him into his room," Tom said over his shoulde

Meredith hurried to the nearest bathroom, where there was a first-aid kit under the sink. Once she had it, she made her way back to Greg's room. When she stepped back into the hallway, Scott and Rachel were nowhere in sight. She assumed they'd gone back to the bridal suite.

Greg was sitting on the edge of his bed, Tom hovering nearby. Meredith moved to the side of the bed and set down the first-aid kit, opening it to pull out some disinfectant. "Do you want some pain relievers?"

"More than anything in the world," he groaned.

"I'll get some water," Tom offered.

"No need." Greg motioned toward the bedside table. A half-empty bottle of water sat on the top. "There's some right here."

Opening a bottle of pain relievers, Meredith shook a couple of pills onto her hand and held them out to him. "I'm just glad you're not asking for something stronger."

"I already agreed you were probably right about me cutting back," he muttered. "You don't have to rub it in."

As he popped the pills in his mouth and reached for the water, she gave a glance around the room, checking to see if he had any alcohol in here he might turn to when they were gone. Mixing alcohol, painkillers and a head injury seemed like a recipe for disaster.

She didn't spot any bottles, empty or otherwise. Not that that necessarily meant anything. Still, it was all she could hope for. And of course, she still had the flask she'd taken from him yesterday.

"Scott said you told him you stopped drinking," Tom said.

"I did. Mostly," he amended a few seconds later. "I make exceptions for special occasions."

"I don't think it's supposed to work that way," Tom replied.

"If you can't drink at a wedding, when can you?" Greg scoffed. "We were supposed to be celebrating this weekend. I know that seems like a long time ago, but that's what we came here for." His voice softened. "At least I thought that's what we came here for," he murmured.

Having dabbed some disinfectant on a cloth, Meredith stood behind Greg. "Can you turn for me a little?" He complied, shifting slightly on the edge of the bed so she could fully see the back of his head. "This might sting," she warned.

"As long as it's not as bad as a candlestick to the head, I think I'll be fine."

"Now are you going to take what's happening here seriously?" Meredith couldn't help asking.

"I always took it seriously," he said, his voice unexpectedly somber.

"Really?" Tom asked, skepticism heavy in his voice. "You sure didn't act like it."

"What should I have done, Tom? Started yelling and screaming my head off like Jess? That didn't work so well for her, did it?" He shrugged. "I'm not afraid of death, Meredith. It's just something that happens."

"What about your family? Your parents? Relatives? Wouldn't they miss you?"

He grew quiet. "Yes. Losing a child. That's not something any parent could get over…. But my parents are both dead, and I don't have any family left. So no, nobody would miss me."

"I didn't know," Tom said softly. "About your parents."

"Yes, well, you've been gone for a long time, Tom," Greg said wryly. "There's a lot you don't know."

As she started to wrap a bandage around Greg's head, Meredith glanced over at Tom in time to see him wince, and she knew the comment had stung.

"I'm sorry," Tom said. "You're right. I wish I'd been here. I should have been a better friend."

Greg shrugged one shoulder. "Nothing you could have done about it. And you have your own life. We all do."

Despite his casual tone, Meredith finally heard what she should have guessed was beneath the partying attitude and copious drinking. Greg was deeply sad.

She cleared her throat, unsure how to respond to the realization, not knowing what to say. She finally pulled her hands back, shifting away from him to deposit the antiseptic and unused bandages back in the kit. "There we go. All done."

"Great," he said with a cheeriness she could now hear was forced.

"Can we get you anything else?"

"I just need to rest for a while," he said. "And lock my door."

"That's not a bad idea," Tom said.

"Let me know if you want me to send up dinner," Meredith offered.

"That won't be necessary," Greg replied with a brief grin. "It'll take a little more than a candlestick to the head to keep me down."

Unfortunately, as they all knew too well, there were far worse threats out there with the potential to keep him down permanently.

Leaving him to rest, Tom and Meredith stepped into the hallway, closing the door behind them.

"What do you think?" Tom asked as she moved back toward the bathroom.

"I don't know," she admitted. "Why would someone hit him in the head and not kill him?"

"Whoever did it could have heard us coming, or gotten scared before they could do anything."

"But neither Haley nor Jessica were hit in the back of the head." As soon as she said it, she frowned, reconsidering. They'd never actually examined the back of either body. "Or were they?"

"I don't know," Tom said. "We didn't look. They might have been. It could explain why no one heard either of them scream."

Meredith stepped into the bathroom, putting the first-aid kit back under the sink as she considered the issue. Returning to the hall, she met his eyes. "We could always check," she suggested quietly.

"We could," he allowed, sounding as excited about the idea as she was.

"Scott and Rachel were each alone," Meredith pointed out carefully, not sure how he would react to the suggestion.

He didn't immediately jump to defend either of them. Instead he sighed, dragging a hand over his face wearily. "I know," he conceded.

"Do you want to talk to them?"

"We probably should—"

The sound of a door opening cut him off. They looked up just in time to see Alex step into the hallway.

He didn't notice them at first, stopping to pull the door shut behind him. Once he turned away from it, he looked up, immediately spotting them. He tensed, eyeing them warily. "Everything all right?"

"No," Tom said flatly. "Someone attacked Greg. Hit him in the back of the head."

Alex's eyes narrowed, as if he wasn't sure he believed him. "Is he okay?"

"He should be. Nothing too serious." He nodded toward the room Alex had just exited. "Have you been in there for a while?"

"Since lunch."

"Did you hear anything?"

"No. Why?"

Tom motioned toward the hallway. "It happened right here. We heard Greg yell out from the stairs at the other end. Seems strange you didn't hear it when you were a lot closer."

Alex shrugged. "I drifted off. I'm a pretty heavy sleeper. Probably not a surprise I didn't hear anything."

"So you weren't downstairs a half an hour ago, either?"

"No, I told you I was in my room for the past several hours."

"So you did," Tom said noncommittally.

Alex eyed the two of them. "Why? Did something else happen?"

"Someone knocked me down," Meredith answered. "Tried to take my keys."

"Did you see who it was?"

She shook her head. "No."

Alex zeroed in on Tom. "And you thought it might be me?"

"I had to ask," Tom said with a complete lack of apology. "You of all people should understand that."

"Oh, I do." To his credit, he didn't appear the slightest bit offended. "Did you check where Rachel was during all of this?"

"In her room," Tom said.

"With Scott?"

Meredith hesitated, remembering the sight of Rachel coming out of their room while Scott had appeared at the stairs. Tom didn't answer immediately, either, a fact that Alex didn't miss.

His eyebrows shot up. "I'm going to take that as a no."

"It seems that Scott went downstairs to get Rachel some water while she waited in their room," Meredith explained.

"So she was up here, alone, not far from where Greg was supposedly hit. Interesting."

Meredith studied the man closely, taking in the shrewdness in his face. "You really don't like her, do you?"

"Not particularly. I remember the way she dropped him like he was nothing to her, all because she said he was neglecting her, wasn't spending enough time for her. The guy was working his ass off, and all she cared about was that he didn't have time for her." He shook his head. "How much of a spoiled brat do you have to be to do something like that? Do you really think somebody like that is going to change? And should Scott really trust somebody who would treat him like that?"

"If that's how you feel, then why did you agree to perform their wedding?" Tom asked.

"Scott asked me," Alex said in a tone that seemed to indicate that explained everything. "They needed someone to do it, and he knew I'd officiated my cousin's wedding. Rachel wanted to get married here in the middle of nowhere. It was impossible to get a minister to travel all this way, and he didn't want a local to do it, a stranger neither of them knew who didn't know them, either. So I said yes."

"You really think she could be involved in this?"

His brow went up again. "You don't?" he asked with thinly concealed disbelief. "She's the one who wanted to come here. She's the one who forced us to drive all the way here in a blizzard when most of us wanted to check into a hotel for the night instead of trekking up a mountain. She did everything she could to bring us to this castle of death." A beat later, he glanced at her. "No offense, Meredith."

"None taken," she murmured. She couldn't exactly defend Sutton Hall given the circumstances, even if she were at all inclined to at the moment.

"It's a big leap from someone being a spoiled brat to being a killer," Tom pointed out.

"Possibly," Alex said. "But someone could still be both."

"It almost sounds like you're out to get her," Meredith said.

"If she's the killer, then yes, I am," Alex said, the coldness in his voice sending a chill down her spine. "There's a reason I do what I do, Meredith. If there's one thing I learned a long time ago, it's that people who do something wrong deserve to be punished." He reached down and placed his hand on his thigh. She recognized it as an unconscious gesture, the same way she sometimes found herself flexing her broken hand without realizing it. She remembered that was the leg he limped on slightly, the one that had been hurt when he'd been struck by the hit-and-run driver.

A brief wince flashed across his face before he cleared it. "Because when they're not," he continued, "When there's no justice, it hurts. It really does." He looked at her, the hardness in his expression sending a sudden tremor of unease quaking through her. "People deserve justice. And the only way for that to happen is for the truth to come out."

TOM STOPPED IN front of the closed door of Scott and Rachel's room, bracing himself before knocking.

"You okay?" Meredith asked beside him. "I can do this if it bothers you."

"No," he said. He needed to see Scott's face when the questions were asked. If anyone would know if he was lying, it was Tom.

Drawing himself up, he knocked on the door.

"Who is it?" a voice asked from the other side. It was Scott.

"Tom and Meredith."

A few seconds passed before the door was opened

slightly, revealing Scott on the other side. He eyed them, clear caution in his gaze. "What's going on?"

"Can we talk to you and Rachel?" Tom asked.

Scott glanced between the two of them, as though expecting to somehow read on their faces what it was they wanted, before finally pulling the door open all the way. "Sure."

Tom stepped aside to let Meredith enter first, then followed her in. He heard Scott shut the door behind them.

As soon as Tom saw the inside of the room, he understood why Meredith had put them in it. It was twice as big as his or any of the others he'd seen, comprising a full suite. The bedroom portion opened into a sitting area in front of a large fireplace. Rachel sat in one of the chairs there. She looked at them expectantly, clearly having heard their brief conversation with Scott at the door.

"What is it?" she asked.

Scott moved to stand behind Rachel's chair, allowing Tom to face the both of them.

"I hate to have to ask this," Tom said. "We were wondering where each of you was in the past hour or so."

"I've been in here the whole time," Rachel said.

"I told you I went down to get Rachel a bottle of water," Scott said.

"How long were you out of the room?"

"I don't know. Maybe twenty, twenty-five minutes."

Tom couldn't help frowning at that, his brow furrowing. That didn't seem right. Sutton Hall was big, but it didn't take that long to get to the kitchen from here.

"It took you that long to make it to the kitchen and back?" Meredith asked, her voice heavy with doubt.

"I took my time," Scott said, a hint of tightness—or defensiveness?—creeping into his voice. "There didn't seem to be any reason to hurry."

Tom did his best to hide his skepticism. With a killer on

the loose, it didn't seem likely anyone would want to take their time wandering the halls on their own. Especially since Scott should have been worried about leaving Rachel alone in the room....

Then Tom slowly registered what he hadn't before. The way Scott and Rachel were both holding themselves a little stiffly. The way neither of them acknowledged each other.

Things were tense between them, the feeling heavy in the air. That was why Scott had taken his time.

If he can be believed, Tom forced himself to concede.

Tom studied the face of one of his oldest friends in the world, one of the closest—if not *the* closest—friends he'd ever had. Could he really believe Scott was capable of hitting Meredith? Of bashing Greg in the back of the head? Or so much worse?

His automatic response was no. He forced himself to ignore it, to really consider the possibility as he took in Scott's familiar face.

Every instinct still said no, even if a whisper of doubt lurked at the edges of his mind.

"Is this about what happened to Greg?" Rachel asked. "Do you actually think one of us hit him?"

"I don't know," Tom said honestly. "But I have to ask."

"Maybe you should ask Alex," Rachel said with a touch of bitterness. "He's the one who seems to have all the answers."

"We did," Tom admitted. He figured he was better off not discussing the details of their conversation with Alex. "He said he was in his room the whole time and didn't hear anything."

"Well, that sounds suspicious," Rachel scoffed.

"Didn't you say the same thing?" Meredith pointed out. Rachel slammed her mouth shut, an angry flush rising in her cheeks.

"It's not just what happened to Greg," Tom said. "Someone knocked Meredith down and tried to take her keys."

Two pairs of startled eyes flew to Meredith's face. "Did they get them?" Rachel asked.

"No," Meredith confirmed.

"And you didn't see who it was?" Scott asked.

"No. Whoever it was attacked me from behind."

"I don't know what to tell you, Tom," Scott said. "I didn't hit Greg and I certainly didn't try to take Meredith's keys from her."

"Neither did I," Rachel said firmly, meeting his and Meredith's eyes in turn.

Scott hadn't defended her, Tom realized, a cold trickle sliding down his spine. He'd defended himself, but not Rachel. It was a far cry from his vigorous defense of her last night, when he said he hadn't even had to consider the question of whether she was involved in the murders. Did it mean anything? Was he starting to doubt her? Or was he simply letting her confirm her own innocence since she'd been alone in the room and he couldn't honestly say she hadn't done it?

Tom simply didn't know, and that disturbed him most of all.

He was probably overanalyzing the moment, but it didn't matter. Because looking at Scott's face, Tom had no idea what he was thinking, the face of his old friend suddenly seeming more mysterious than ever before.

Chapter Sixteen

The group that assembled for dinner was understandably subdued. Tom eyed the others, taking in the grim faces and downcast eyes. Scott and Rachel sat next to each other but didn't so much as glance in each other's direction. Greg's head was still bandaged. Alex looked up from his plate every once in a while to shoot glances at the others before dropping his head again.

Meredith and Ellen had just begun placing the meal on the table when Rick walked into the dining room. "Ms. Sutton—" He came to an abrupt stop once he saw the scene in front of him. "I'm sorry. Don't mean to interrupt…"

"It's all right, Rick," Meredith said, straightening to face him. "What is it?"

"Just wanted to let you know I managed to get the plow hooked up to the truck. I tested it and it's good to go. I can start trying to clear the road in the morning."

Tom felt a trace of guilt for having left Rick to finish with the plow on his own. But after what had happened to Meredith, he hadn't wanted to let her out of his sight even for a moment. And he hadn't.

"Why wait until then?" Rachel asked. "Can't you get started now so we can get out of here sooner?"

Rick gave his head a tight shake. "Too dangerous trying to navigate that winding mountain road in just the lights from the plow. The snow's so high I won't be able to see anything else. I'd rather to wait until daylight when I can see better, especially since it's my first time trying to do it."

As Tom listened to the man's words, he had to frown. He was the one who'd driven a plow before, a remnant of his childhood growing up in Minnesota. The job would go faster if a more experienced driver were operating the plow. Not to mention it probably would be better if there was more than one person doing the job—two pairs of eyes to keep a look out on that treacherous, winding mountain road, another pair of hands if something went wrong. Anything to get them out—and the police in here—faster.

Then he glanced at Meredith, the words dying on his lips.

If he was with Rick working on clearing the road, Meredith would be here in the house alone.

With the killer.

A chill swept over him, every part of him recoiling at the idea. He couldn't leave her. Not after today. The memory of how she'd looked lying on the floor, the terror that had ripped through him, all came rushing back. No, if there was even a chance of it happening again...

He looked around the table for any other options. "Rick, do you need any help?" he asked, gauging the others' reactions.

Rick appeared to consider the question. "It couldn't hurt. Might get the job done faster."

No one else at the table gave any indication they'd picked up on the hint. But then, with his head injury and likely self-medication, Greg was in no condition to help. Even if things were tense between them, Scott wouldn't want to leave Rachel for that long, and Tom wouldn't have felt right asking him to do it. Alex made no move to volunteer. He shot Rick a suspicious look before lowering his eyes.

Considering the wary glance Rick shot across the table,

he didn't particularly want to work with any of them, either. Of course, Tom thought, swallowing a groan. After today, any suspicions he'd had toward Rick were gone, and Rick seemed to trust him, too. But as far as he knew, one of the others was a killer. Any of the others who were innocent might suspect the same of him. None of them would want to work together and be alone for long stretches at a time.

That left Tom.

He looked at Meredith. She stood biting her lip, apparently deep in thought. Most likely she was also considering her options, not feeling right asking one of her guests for their help, especially after all they'd been through.

He needed to do something to get her—get all of them—out of here.

He forced himself to swallow his ambivalence. "I'll help you," he told Rick. "We can get started first thing."

He would just have to make sure Meredith was safe while they worked.

AFTER AN INCREDIBLY tense dinner, the guests quickly retreated to their rooms. Rick headed to bed, exhausted from the work he'd done that day and needing to get some rest for the big day ahead of him tomorrow. Ellen finished cleaning up the kitchen, then accepted Meredith's offer to fill the dishwasher, retreating to her own room.

Meredith and Tom were left in the kitchen, working in silence. She'd noticed that he hadn't said much at dinner, so she didn't try to get him to talk. They all had a lot on their minds.

There was something comfortable about being with him, doing something as mundane as loading a dishwasher together. She tried not to read too much into it, didn't want to make more of it than it was. It was nice. No more, no less.

And after everything that had happened over the past few days, a nice, quiet moment was more than enough.

When they were finished, they made their way out of the kitchen, shutting off the lights, heading back to the main foyer. It was still early, but Sutton Hall was silent and tranquil.

Unsurprisingly, no one was up for wandering the halls.

"Thank you for volunteering to help Rick," Meredith said softly as they climbed the staircase to the second floor. "I think everybody is happy to be getting out of here sooner— and to have the police finally arrive."

"Somebody had to do it," he said flatly. "I just wish it didn't have to be me."

"I know it's going to be a lot of work, and I would do it if I could, but I wouldn't feel right leaving Ellen and the rest of the wedding party alone in the house. Not when we don't know who the killer is. I need to be here for them. I have to do my best to make sure nothing else happens."

They'd reached the second-floor landing. As expected, the hallway was empty.

He looked over at her in amazement. "I don't care how much work it's going to be. I hate the idea of leaving *you* alone in the house. I don't want anything to happen to you."

Irritated, she shot him a glare. "I told you I don't need a babysitter."

"And I told you I wasn't saying you need one. But everybody can use somebody to watch their back, especially with a killer on the loose."

"I can take care of myself," she told him firmly. They'd reached his room. Expecting him to stop, she picked up speed, continuing on toward her room.

To her surprise, he fell into step beside her. "I can't believe I care more about your safety than you do."

"You don't."

"It sure seems that way."

They arrived in front of her door. With nowhere else to go, she stopped, whirling to face him. "Is this because you feel sorry for me? Because of what happened with Brad? Because I don't need your pity."

"Is that what you think?" he asked with a combination of amusement and disbelief. "I don't want anything to happen to you because I feel *sorry* for you?"

It did sound kind of foolish when he said it like that. "Then what is it? I don't see you getting this protective with anyone else."

He looked at her for a long moment, something in that steady gaze setting off a nervous flutter in her belly. "You really don't know?" he asked, his voice suddenly softer.

He moved closer, forcing her to tilt her head up to meet his eyes. Only a step separated them, maybe less. She didn't look to see. She couldn't. She could only stare into his eyes and the unexpected heat she saw simmering in them.

Deep down she felt a whisper of disbelief, the doubt of that girl she'd once been, unable to fathom that she could possibly be seeing what she thought she did in Tom Campbell's eyes.

But she wasn't that girl anymore. And he wasn't that boy. He was a man now, a man standing mere inches away, a man looking at her as no man ever had.

The man who wanted her.

A thrill raced through her, exploding along her nerve endings at the certainty, the absolute firmness of that knowledge inside her, just before he lowered his mouth to hers.

The kiss was soft, gentle. His lips brushed against hers with the sweetest caress, strong and sure and lingering. Her eyelids automatically drifted shut as the feeling of that achingly sweet contact washed over her. At the same time, her lips instinctively parted. His immediately moved against them again, then again, gradually deepening the kiss. His tongue dived forth into her mouth to claim her, driving a moan from deep in her throat. He cupped the back of her head in his hand, his fingertips stroking against her skin, drawing her mouth closer to him, devouring her further.

Suddenly her back bumped against the door behind her. Something hard dug into her spine.

The doorknob, she realized, wincing against the pain.

He must have noticed. He immediately broke the kiss. A deep sense of loss crashed over her and it was all she could do not to reach out and catch his face in her hands, to pull him back to her. He leaned away slightly, his face still only inches from hers.

The distance allowed her to see what was behind him. The empty hallway. She suddenly remembered where they were, what lurked in the shadows. She glanced down the hall. "We shouldn't do this," she whispered. "Not here."

"You're right," he murmured, releasing her. He scanned the hall, as well.

She watched him, wondering what would happen next, what she wanted to happen next.

And she knew. Knew exactly what she wanted to happen, more than anything she'd ever wanted in her entire life.

She reached into her pocket and pulled out her keys, quickly unlocking the door. Shoving it open, she stepped inside and turned back to face him.

He stood just on the other side of the threshold, watching her, seemingly waiting to see what she wanted to do.

Meredith pushed the door open farther and took another step back.

"Are you sure about this?" he asked softly.

"Yes." People were dying all around them. They didn't know when they would get out of here, didn't know what would happen next, didn't know if they could count on seeing tomorrow. All the more reason to live for the moment, for now.

She needed this. She needed him.

"I don't want to be alone tonight."

He didn't hesitate further, walking into the room and pushing the door shut behind him.

Then, finally, his mouth was on hers again. She plunged her hands into his hair to hold him close, to draw him near as his lips stroked against hers, as she met him kiss for kiss. Each one only drove the need inside her higher. Each one was better than the last. She needed them. She needed this. She needed more. She needed to touch him, to taste him. Needed the utterly, achingly delicious feeling of his tongue moving against hers, of his mouth capturing, taking, teasing her own.

She felt his hands go around her hips. They reached for the bottom of her sweater, his fingertips brushing the soft skin at the small of her back.

She instinctively tensed.

As soon as she did she wished she hadn't. Because Tom went still, clearly having felt her reaction. A moment later, he pulled away. She felt a burst of fear that he would let her go entirely.

He didn't, leaning back just far enough to look into her eyes, an open question in his.

"Everything okay?"

Meredith nodded quickly. Her cheeks burned with humiliation. "Yes. I'm sorry. It's just…I haven't…been with anyone since…" She swallowed hard.

She saw from his face that she didn't need to finish. He knew what she meant.

Since Brad.

His voice gentled. "We don't have to do this…."

The warmth, the kindness, the sheer tenderness on that

magnificent face broke something inside her. That momentary uncertainty vanished, washed away in a rush of adrenaline that poured through her.

She held on tightly to the front of his sweater, not wanting to let him get even an inch farther away. "Yes," she said over the lump in her throat. "The past few days have been a nightmare. The past year— Heck, the past seven years were so terrible it's felt like I would never wake up from them. I've had the nightmare. Now I want the dream."

She watched the words wash over him, saw the shifting emotions as they sank in. Finally his expression softened. A slight smile touched his lips, just before he lowered them to hers once more.

It was just a single kiss. He pressed his lips to hers firmly, catching her mouth in one long, lingering caress before breaking it off. His smile deepening, he eased her fingers from his sweater.

"Why don't I start?"

Reaching down, he tore off his sweater, revealing a lean, toned torso dusted with blond hair. The breath hitched in her throat as she took in the sight of him. It was the body of an active man, long and lightly muscled. She instinctively reached out, wanting to feel the warmth of his skin, the coiled strength beneath it. And then her hand was there, on his chest. She basked in the sight of it, relished the sensation of it, as an ineffable giddiness swirled through her. His chest hair was soft beneath her fingers. His heat soaked into her palm, sliding up her arm to fill her to the core with his warmth.

It was amazing. It was indescribable.

It wasn't enough.

She wanted to feel all of him. She wanted to feel every part of him pressed against every part of her.

With some reluctance, she pulled her hand away, dropping it to the bottom of her own sweater. Taking a breath, she pulled it off, letting it tumble from her fingers to the floor.

She watched him as his gaze moved over her, the blueness of his eyes deepening, with desire, with approval. He slowly raised his hand toward her. She tried to quell the tremor of nervousness that quaked through her, even as she couldn't tell how much of it was nervousness and how much was actually excitement. She expected him to reach for her bra, to unhook it, to release her breasts.

He didn't. He reached out and placed his hand on her side, just above her hip. The touch was gentle, careful, his skin warm and soft. He kept his hand there, unmoving, and she realized what he was doing. Letting her adjust to the feeling, to his touch. Fresh heat spilled through her at the tenderness of it, at the kindness.

She reached out, wrapping her arms around his neck, and caught his mouth with hers. Their lips moved together again, faster, hungrier. She felt his hands move against her back, stroking against her skin. At some point he must have unhooked her bra. Suddenly the garment was slipping away. Her breasts were free, pressed against the hard wall of his chest, her sensitive nipples brushing against his chest hair. The feeling of his bare skin on hers was good. So very good. It just reminded her how much she'd wanted it, how much she'd wanted more.

She fumbled for the button of his pants. Simultaneously, she felt his hands at her waistband. They shoved out of their pants, kicking them off, casting aside their underwear. And then she felt it, all of him, his thighs against hers, their hips meeting, the hard length of his erection pressing against her, eager, insistent.

He suddenly bent, scooping her up into his arms. Then he was lowering her onto the bed. Turning away, he reached for his pants on the floor, allowing her to see all of him, everything that had been pressed against her only moments ago. He looked every bit as good as he felt. She could have stared all night, the ache inside her pounding harder, heavier, with every glance. She'd thought he was beautiful before. The full view was only better.

He pulled out his wallet and retrieved a foil packet. Within moments he'd covered himself and returned to her. Lowering himself onto the bed, he stretched out beside her, his hands immediately reaching for her, hungrily, eagerly, as though he couldn't get enough of touching her. She couldn't keep her hands off him any more than he could, her fingers skimming over every hard ridge of his belly, glancing over the wide expanse of his shoulders, reaching out to grasp his erection and stroke the silky hardness, feeling it surge against her fingers. Until it wasn't enough.

As soon as she thought it, he rolled her over onto her back, moving with her to position himself above her. She braced herself for that burst of fear at having someone on top of her, ready to shake it off as soon as it happened, not about to let it ruin this.

It never came. As he moved on top of her and braced himself above her, all she felt was the rightness of it. Of being here with him. Of what was about to happen next.

He looked down into her eyes, a question amidst the cloudy desire in his.

She answered it with a smile, raising her hips, urging him forward.

He needed no further prompting. He pushed his hips forward, sliding into her, burying himself to the hilt.

And it was utterly perfect. More than she could have dreamed. The rightness of having this man with her, inside her, above her.

As he moved inside her, she peered up into his face, taking in the beauty of it. He was still the most beautiful man she'd ever seen, even more so now that she knew who he was inside, the man beneath the flawless exterior.

And found him staring back at her, his deep blue eyes focused intently on her face, like he couldn't get enough of looking at her.

Like she was beautiful, too.

Happiness soared through her in a rush and she smiled, unable to keep the feeling off her face. He returned it, his lips widening in a big, open grin, and kissed her again.

Their bodies moved in tandem, building in rhythm and speed, matching the growing intensity of the emotions pounding through her. There was so much. Arousal and desire and need. Excitement and happiness and wonder. The feeling of all of them clashing together was heady, intense, a giddy swirl of so many emotions and sensations building inside her, the pressure growing. She couldn't breathe. It was too much. Each moment built to more, more pleasure, more wonder, more everything. Until finally she couldn't take it any longer. She erupted, feeling him explode with her, in her, around her at the same moment, in a flood of sensation.

And as they came down together and she clung to him, basking in every moment, she felt one thing above all else.

Joy.

"As if I didn't hate the idea of leaving you enough already…"

Curled up by Tom's side, her cheek resting on his chest, Meredith smiled. "I hate it, too, but it has to be done. The phones are still down. The only way we're going to get out of here is to get the road cleared."

He exhaled, his breath brushing over the top of her head.

"I know. But there has to be a way of keeping you safe when I'm not here…."

The delicious warmth of what they'd just shared began to fade. Here they were again. Back to this.

She understood the motivation behind the words, knew that he genuinely cared about her, but they still rankled. "I told you, I'm just going to have to take care of myself. I know I didn't do the best job of it today," she added quickly when she felt him start to interrupt, "but I'll just have to be more careful. I can do this. I *have* to do this."

"Why?" he asked, his frustration clear. "Why do you *have* to do this on your own? I wouldn't want to be on my own in a situation like this with no one having my back."

"But you would do it if you had to, wouldn't you? And I bet no one would question your ability to."

"That's not what I'm doing—"

"Yes, it is. And I can't depend on you or Adam or anyone else to save me." Even she could hear the note of desperation in the words and wished she could take them back.

He was silent for a long moment. "This isn't really about me not thinking you can take of yourself, is it? It's about proving it to yourself."

She couldn't answer, the admission too humiliating.

"What is this really about? Brad?"

Damn. She should have known he'd figure it out. "I can't be that weak again," she whispered. "I can't."

He fell quiet again. When he finally spoke, his voice was rough. "You said you were married to Brad for four years. How much of that time was he hurting you?"

Meredith sucked in a breath against the sudden onslaught of memories. "He always had a temper, but we'd been married about six months the first time he hit me."

From his silence, he was letting that piece of information sink in. "Why didn't you leave him sooner?" he asked, his voice rough.

A lump lodged her throat. She knew the answer. She'd spent plenty of time thinking about those years and her own motivations during them. That didn't mean it was any easier to admit.

She had to force the words out. "Because I loved him." She nearly winced, knowing how stupid and pathetic and utterly absurd that had to sound. "I know that doesn't make sense. How could anyone love somebody who'd do that... who'd treat them like that? But I did. He was everything to me. From the first time I saw him I was amazed that somebody that handsome and confident would be interested in me." She swallowed against the humiliation she could feel climbing in her throat. "Sometimes I wonder how much I felt for him was just awe. I never thought someone like that would give me the time of day, and when he did, there was a part of me that was just pathetically grateful for the attention."

"Why wouldn't he have given you the time of day?"

"He was way, way out of my league." She shook her head. "You don't remember him, what he looked like."

"I don't need to. I know what you look like."

She started to shake her head. "You don't have to say that—"

"I know I don't. And I'm not just saying it." He reached down and caught her chin with his forefinger, tilted her face up to peer into her eyes. "Have I given you any reason to doubt that I think you're an incredibly sexy woman?" A grin touched his lips, his blue eyes darkening with desire. "Because if I did, I can try harder."

Her leg was slung over his, and against her thigh she felt the growing proof of his arousal.

"I believe you." She smiled. "But that's how I felt. How

I always felt around him. And since I never really felt like I was good enough, it was easier to accept that when he got angry it was my fault. And those times when he did look at me and smile, I was always so happy, and I'd forget how awful and terrifying he could be. Everything seemed worth it when he smiled or seemed happy, like I had done something right, like he was happy with me. If he wasn't, I would just have to try harder, and then everything would be okay."

"But it wasn't."

"No," she admitted quietly.

"What made you finally leave?"

She swallowed hard. "I was in the hospital. Brad…he broke my jaw and a couple of bones in my face. And I had some bruised ribs. I couldn't talk, couldn't really move. Mrs. Hagerty, our neighbor, found me. She knew what had been happening, had tried to get me to do something, but…I didn't. When she didn't see me leave the house that morning, she came over. She called an ambulance and they took me to the hospital. They kept me overnight for a few days. And even then, I remember lying in that hospital bed wondering what was wrong with me, why I couldn't make him happy. Why he couldn't love me enough not to…" The words stuck in her throat.

"It wasn't your fault," Tom said fiercely. "It was that bastard's."

"I know that. Now," she added faintly. She cleared her throat. "Adam, my brother, found out. I hadn't told him about any of it, hadn't wanted to admit what had been happening. I think subconsciously I knew he would have tried to get me out and I still wanted Brad. But when I was in the hospital, Adam tried to get in touch with me. Brad wouldn't tell him where I was, but he managed to reach Mrs. Hagerty, who did."

She pulled in a ragged breath. "I still remember when

he came into my room and saw me for the first time. He didn't even look angry. He was just…devastated. He actually started to cry, and if you ever met Adam he's the last guy you'd ever expect to cry. I had never seen him do that before. And I remembered I did have somebody who loved me.

"He got me out of there and we stayed in a hotel while I recovered. He wouldn't let me go home, even to pick up my belongings. I think he was afraid Brad might try to convince me to stay, and if that failed, get violent again. He was probably right. He took care of that for me. Got what I wanted from the house for me. Found me an attorney. He saved me when I couldn't save myself."

She swallowed the hard lump that had formed in her throat. "I guess I'm just that weak."

His arm tightened around her, drawing her closer to him. "Maybe you were, but you're not now."

She exhaled softly. "I don't know about that."

"Are you kidding? 'Weak' is the last thing I would call the woman who's been in charge here the past several days."

Doubt flickered through her. "I was just doing what I had to."

"Isn't that what strong people do?"

She'd never thought of it that way. Maybe it really was just as simple as that. "I guess so."

He brushed a kiss against the top of her head. "I'm glad you got away," he said roughly, his voice thick with emotion.

She turned her face into his chest, deeply breathing in the scent of him. No matter what happened after this terrible weekend, she would never forget this—the smell that was purely, distinctively his, the way his body felt, the sound of his voice softened with tenderness and the rumble of his heartbeat. She closed her eyes, grateful to have had this moment. "Me, too," she whispered.

"I still hate the idea of leaving you."

At the moment she wasn't particularly looking forward to that, either. "Guess I'll just have to be strong, right?"

She felt him smile. "I'm not worried about that," he said. "But whoever is doing this is clearly dangerous. If they do come after you, you might not be able to fight them off again, especially since they know what to expect now. You could be hurt. Or worse…"

The words cut off abruptly. His body tensed against her, as though even talking about the possibility bothered him.

"If the killer does have another target, then the fact that we could be getting out of here soon might make them act again, before their intended victim can get away or the police arrive to stop them."

He was right. The killer had purposely, deliberately come here with a plan to kill people. The same person who'd brought the knives to accomplish that mission wasn't going to stop until that mission was completed.

"So I need to make it impossible for them to do that."

"But how are you going to do that?"

An idea suddenly sparked in her mind. Excitement rushing through her, she smiled slowly. "You want somebody looking out for me? Well, I know exactly who it should be."

"Who?"

"All of them."

Chapter Seventeen

When the wedding party shuffled into the dining room for breakfast the next morning, the first thing Meredith noticed was how small the group was. There were so few of them, she noted with a pang. Only four of them—Scott and Rachel, Alex and Greg—taking their seats at one end of the massive table.

Maybe she should ask if they'd like to eat in the kitchen, she thought. A smaller table and more intimate setting might make it less obvious how much smaller their group was now. But by the time it occurred to her, they were already taking their seats.

She mustered a smile. "Good morning." She received a few muttered greetings in reply.

"Tom come down yet?" Scott asked, glancing around the room.

"He and Rick left already," she said. "They were up early to get started with the plow. Tom tried it out and said the snow isn't packed too hard. He's hopeful they might actually get the road cleared by the end of the day."

It was a lie, a necessary one to sell them on her plan. As long as they thought they wouldn't be here much longer, it would work better. Tom and Rick would just reveal at the end of the day that it was taking longer than they'd expected.

As anticipated, the group seemed to perk up at the news.

She examined the smiling faces closely, searching for the slightest indication any of them wasn't as excited as they should be. All she saw was the expected relief.

She quickly served the meal and waited until they'd started eating before speaking again. "I wanted to talk to you all about something," she announced, drawing their attention. "I was thinking it might be best if we all stayed in the living room today. I know you all have to be sick of staying in your rooms and it's not really safe to be wandering around alone. There are plenty of books and magazines, and you can bring down any laptops or tablets. We can all watch out for each other, even protect each other if we need to, though it'll be much less likely with all of us together. Safety in numbers, that kind of thing."

"Wouldn't we be safer in our rooms?" Alex asked.

"You can't stay in your rooms all day," Meredith pointed out. "The two of you—" she nodded to Alex and Greg "—don't have bathrooms in your rooms, so you have to leave them several times during the day anyway. And then there are mealtimes. Every moment you're alone is a moment you're vulnerable. If we all stick together the whole time, nothing should be able to happen."

She paused. "Unless there's a reason any of you wouldn't want the rest of us knowing where you are or what you're doing...."

She saw from the narrowing of more than a few eyes that they got the implication—and didn't like it one bit. They also couldn't argue about it without looking suspicious.

The exceptions were Scott and Rachel, who could claim that they were better off in their room together, where they were already watching out for each other. Meredith waited for one—or both—of them to make the point.

Neither did. They both remained silent, as she'd thought they might. The tension between them was too obvious.

Being around the others instead of sequestered alone together might be a relief at this point.

This time she didn't have to fake her smile. "Great," she said. "Then it's settled."

This is going to work, she assured herself as the wedding party began to eat again. With everyone in the same room, she would be able to watch over them, and they would be able to protect each other, if the killer was foolish enough to try something with all of them there.

Or crazy enough, she amended. Because being together didn't just mean she'd know where they all were. It meant the killer would be there, too. A killer who might not be willing to let anything stop him—or her—from completing whatever evil plan they had in mind.

And it was up to her most of all to make sure nothing happened.

BY NOON, MEREDITH was beginning to suspect the day would never end.

Once she'd gotten the group assembled in the living room, she'd built a roaring fire in the stone fireplace. Under different circumstances the room would have felt comfortable, cozy. Instead it was nearly unbearable, the air charged with tension, the silence absolute.

Looking up from her notepad, she scanned the group. They'd all moved to separate areas of the room, occupying themselves with various gadgets and types of reading material. No one had said much of anything to one another in hours. She'd thought she sensed a few stolen glances, but hadn't been able to look fast enough to determine who they'd come from or been directed toward.

At least they were alive and safe, Meredith thought. For that, she would endure the oppressive quiet that blanketed the room and crackling uneasiness in the air. Besides, it would be lunch before long. That would offer a brief, much-needed reprieve.

She lowered her gaze back to the pad in her lap. As soon as she saw what was on the paper, she flinched slightly. She'd been drawing without really paying attention to what she'd been doing, the impulse instinctive, her thoughts focused elsewhere. On the multitude of questions in her head. On keeping an eye on the group. On how long it might take to clear the road and how soon the police might arrive…

All while her subconscious had been focused on something else. Or someone.

Tom's face peered up at her from the paper.

It was a good likeness, she had to admit. As she took in the image, her heartbeat kicked up, almost as if she was looking at the man himself. It wasn't just the face, but the expression on it, that was instantly recognizable.

It was how he'd looked last night, peering down at her. His eyes were softened, the look in them intimate and achingly tender.

The memories, the emotions, of what they'd shared came rushing back. She didn't want to read too much into it, didn't want to ruin one of the best memories she'd ever made by trying to make it into something it wasn't. Whatever else happened, she just wanted to cherish it—and never forget.

Staring down at the image she'd drawn, she knew she never would.

Grateful no one could see the sketch, Meredith quickly closed the pad and set it aside.

Restless, she pushed to her feet and walked to the nearest window. There still wasn't much to see, just an unending sea of white. She was hoping to get some glimmer of Tom and Rick. The path they dug from the garage would take them by this side of the house, but she hadn't heard ny signs of the plow and couldn't see any hint of it from his vantage point.

Turning away from the window, her gaze fell on the bar few feet away. She automatically moved toward it, thinking it might give her something to do. She might as well get tarted at clearing out the empty bottles. There was likely o be more than a few after Greg had made his way through he liquor over the past several days.

Stopping in front of the bar, she reached for the nearest ottle and started to pick it up, only to stop and frown at he weight in her hand.

The bottle was full.

Looking closer she saw the seal hadn't even been broken. Evidently Greg wasn't a fan of gin. Sliding the bottle back nto place, she glanced at the bar to see which were empty.

Her frown deepened. None of them were.

All of them were mostly or entirely full.

Meredith stared at the sight in front of her, trying to make ense of what she was seeing.

It didn't make sense. Greg had been drinking for days. He'd visited the bar at least a half dozen times this morning alone. She knew he didn't have any bottles in his room; he'd looked yesterday when she was in there. And he'd said he other day he'd been refilling his flask with vodka, yet f he had, there wouldn't be anywhere near as much left in he bottle.

Unless he hadn't been drinking as much as he'd seemed o be. But then he wouldn't have been as drunk as he'd eemed to be....

He had to have been faking it.

She suddenly remembered that look of fury in his eyes when she'd taken his flask. In the moment, she'd thought was because she'd taken his liquor away from him. Now he had to wonder if there was another reason—because he didn't want her finding out that there wasn't any alcohol in the flask? Or because it was harder to maintain the charade that he was drunk without it?

And it was a charade. She suddenly knew it without doubt. It was all an act to get them to believe…what? That he wasn't a threat? But why—

There was only on explanation she could think of.

Cold, hard certainty settled over her.

It was Greg. Greg was the killer.

She didn't know why. She only knew it had to be true.

"Meredith, is everything all right?"

A jolt ripped through her at the sound of his voice. She wondered if she was imagining the edge she heard in the casually spoken question, if anyone else heard it. He must have noticed how long she'd been standing there without moving, might have guessed what she'd figured out.

Damn. She never had been very good at lying or playing games. She cleared her throat. "Yes, of course. I must have zoned out for a second."

Doing her best to keep her composure, she made herself turn around. She didn't want to look at him, didn't want to risk betraying her thoughts. Then she realized how suspicious that would look, as clear a tip-off as accusing him outright. She forced herself to meet his eyes.

They were fixed firmly on her.

And coolly, chillingly, unmistakably sober.

The corners of his mouth twitched wryly. "You figured it out, didn't you?"

She didn't know what to say. Deep down she recognized that it didn't matter. The answer had to be written all over her face.

The rest of the room seemed to go still, as though the others were realizing something was happening. Meredith sensed eyes shifting from her to Greg and back again.

"What's going on?" Scott asked warily.

Still words escaped her.

"I guess it's over then." Rising to his feet, Greg shrugged lightly. "That's too bad. I was enjoying this."

And with that, he pulled a gun from behind his back and aimed it directly at Rachel.

"Let's finish this."

Chapter Eighteen

A stunned hush fell over the room. All eyes went to Greg—or at least the object gripped in his hand.

A split second later, Scott began to shove up from his chair. "Greg, what the hell—"

"Back off, Scott," Greg ordered without looking at him. "Unless you want me to pull the trigger right now, you'll stay in your seat."

Scott froze half-out of the chair. Meredith could practically feel the physical effort he had to exert not to move any farther. Finally, slowly, furiously, he lowered himself back in his seat.

Meredith frantically tried to think of what to do. Even if he wanted to make a move, Scott was nowhere close to Greg. Alex, too, was on the other side of the room. By the time either of them got across the room, Greg would have fired off a shot, maybe two. Greg had been the one seated closest to Rachel, a choice Meredith suspected had been deliberate.

And now she was closest to both of them.

If anyone was going to stop this, it was going to have to be her.

She took a step forward, trying to draw his attention to her. "So what was in the flask, Greg? Since clearly you weren't filling it with anything from here."

His eyes flicked toward her for the slightest of moments. He smirked. "Water."

"Why not just leave it empty?"

"A guy does get thirsty."

"So what were you doing in here the other day when you told Tom and me you were refilling the flask?"

"Listening in on your conversation. I heard you coming and decided to duck in here so I could hear what you were talking about, in case you'd figured anything out."

"Like you did outside Haley's room?"

The smirk deepened. "Guilty."

"Why pretend to be drinking so much?" she asked, easing ever closer. "Why the charade?"

"I figured it might give me an advantage, make people less likely to suspect me."

"Like a blow to the back of the head?"

"Figured that out, did you? Yes, when I couldn't get your keys I figured I needed another way to get close to these two, to make myself seem innocent. I just didn't get a chance to take advantage of it before you rounded all of us up in here."

The smile evaporated, his expression becoming deadly serious. "Now if you don't mind, I'm going to have to ask you to sit down. This isn't any of your business."

"It looks like you're about to kill someone in my house," she said calmly. "I believe that makes it my business."

"I don't want to have to hurt you."

Meredith almost shook her head in amazement. "You've already killed two people. Don't tell me you're suddenly developing a conscience."

"I don't need to. I don't have anything to feel guilty for. They deserved what happened to them. You don't. But I can't afford to let you stop me from finishing what I came here to do."

She raised her chin, meeting his eyes with an unblinking stare. "So what are you going to do if I don't sit?"

He tilted his head, his mouth twisting in a mocking smile. "Come on, Meredith. You're not fooling anyone. We both know this whole tough-girl routine is just an act. Most of these guys might not have remembered you. I mean, let's face it—you weren't all that memorable. But I do. I remember that girl who used to follow Brad Jackson around like a puppy. I knew Jess was wrong. Brad was a bully with a temper. I had no trouble believing a guy like that would beat his wife. And you would have let him, wouldn't you? Because you're not a fighter. So why don't we make this easy and you sit down and stop wasting both of our time?"

The words struck a painful, familiar chord inside her. Because he was right. She never had been a fighter. She'd always gone with the flow, tried to get along, tried to make people happy. She'd never fought back against her mother's criticisms and derisions. She'd never fought back against Brad, not once. And she *had* let him hurt her, far more than any person should ever let another.

And Greg was also dead wrong. Because she wasn't that person anymore. She was done being treated badly. She was done being dumped on and taking anything she didn't deserve from anyone.

She wasn't weak. Not anymore.

More than anything Tom had said, she finally believed it herself, could feel it in her bones as hard determination surged through her in a powerful rush.

She was strong.

And she would be damned if she let this man hurt anyone again.

"No," she said firmly, her voice hard, not bothering to hide her anger. His eyes flared in surprise, the sight sending a surge of satisfaction through her. "I'm not going to let you hurt anybody else."

"She deserves it."

"People who hurt other people always think they have a reason. That doesn't make it right."

The patronizing amusement on his face only deepened. "And how exactly do you intend to stop me?"

She stepped closer. "Any way I have to."

In an instant, every trace of patronizing amusement vanished from his face, replaced with cold purpose.

And he aimed the gun at her. "Stop."

She did, every limb, every muscle, every cell in her body freezing as she stared at the gun aimed square at her chest.

"I don't want to hurt you," Greg said. "You're not a part of this. But I will if I have to. I think I proved that yesterday with your keys."

"No, you won't."

The words were deadly calm. They also didn't come from anyone in the room, echoing from the doorway.

Her heart leaping, Meredith jerked her head toward the entryway, recognizing that voice before she saw the speaker.

Tom. It was Tom.

He stood there, hands fisted at his sides, every inch of him radiating fury. Rick loomed behind him.

He was here. He was even farther away than Scott, but he was here. Another distraction, another chance to talk Greg out of doing something.

"Put the gun down, Greg," he said evenly, though there was no missing the thread of barely suppressed anger in his voice.

Frowning, Greg barely glanced at him. "I thought you were clearing the road."

"We were. We got as far as we could before we had to turn back to refuel the truck. More important, we were able to get a cell phone signal and get through to the police. They're going to start digging from the other end. They'll be here as soon as they can."

Any triumph Meredith might have felt at the news was killed by the hardness that fell over Greg's features. "Then I guess it really is time for Rachel to get what she deserves." He swung the gun back to her. "One more move from any of you and I pull the trigger. Believe me, there is nothing I want more. The others were just warm-ups for this."

"You killed them," Rachel said in horror and disbelief. "Haley… Jess… You *killed* them."

His face twisted with sudden rage. "No, *you* killed them, the same way you killed my son!"

Rachel stared at him, mouth agape. "What are you talking about?"

"Are you finally ready to stop lying? About the reason you didn't want me invited to this wedding? About why you broke up with Scott back in college?"

Rachel's eyes flared with unmistakable panic.

"I already know why," Scott said flatly. "Kim told me a long time ago."

Rachel jerked her head toward Scott. "She did?"

"Yeah. It's because I didn't have enough money."

Greg arched a brow. "Oh, is that what Kim told you? I'm afraid she was lying, covering for her friend here so you would give up on her and not learn the real reason."

A chilly silence fell over the room. Greg looked at Rachel expectantly.

"Rachel, what is he talking about?" Scott finally asked.

She blinked rapidly. "I…I…"

Greg exhaled sharply, the sound thick with contempt. "You just can't tell the truth, can you? Even now, even after everything that's happened, even when it's clear there's no way it isn't coming out, you refuse to just come clean."

Rachel began to shake, but still she said nothing, her lips working silently, no sound coming out.

"Fine," Greg said, looking straight at Scott. For a split second, a hint of something that almost looked like regret touched his eyes. "Rachel and I slept together in college."

Scott flinched, the color slowly draining from his face. His shocked gaze swung sharply from Rachel to Greg, finally settling back on his fiancée. "Rach, what is he talking about?" he said again.

She looked him straight in the eye, tears brimming in hers. "I'm so sorry."

"How could you do that?" He jerked his head back toward Greg. "How could *either of you* do that?"

Greg had the grace to look chagrined. "Well, I think we all know I didn't always make the best decisions when I'd had a few. That's assuming I even recognized it was her. The sad thing is, I didn't even remember it happened."

"It was a *mistake*," Rachel said, her eyes pleading as she stared at Scott.

"And it was only her first one," Greg said. "Because then she found out she was pregnant."

He stopped dramatically, as though giving Rachel time to deny it.

She didn't, closing her eyes as tears began to stream down her cheeks.

"You…had a baby?" Scott said numbly. "*His* baby?"

Rachel simply sat there, her body shaking, wincing against the words as though they were physical blows.

"I'm assuming the timing didn't work out, so she couldn't try to pass it off as yours," Greg said. "Some women might have gotten rid of it, but not Rachel. Somehow I have a feeling it had more to do with not being able to destroy a part of herself than any kind of maternal love. Because that's all that matters, Rachel, isn't it? You?"

"You don't know anything about it," she ground out through gritted teeth. "You don't know how hard it was."

"How could I, since you never told me? I had to find out from Kim."

"Why?" Scott asked, still staring at Rachel in disbelief. "Why would you sleep with him? We were in love."

"Yes, we were," Rachel said desperately. "We *are*."

Scott's stony silence was as devastating as a straight denial. Rachel flinched.

With all eyes off her, Meredith realized this was her chance to make a move. She couldn't get close enough to Greg, not without him noticing. But she could get between him and Rachel.

Directly in the line of fire.

She began to ease over to her left, slowly, gradually, praying he wouldn't notice.

"It was the end-of-semester party fall of senior year," Rachel explained. "Do you remember? I'd barely seen you all semester. You kept bailing on me and canceling every time we had plans, but you promised you'd be there. It was our last chance to be together before I went home for the winter break. You promised. And then you stood me up. Again.

"I wasn't thinking straight. I was drinking, and I was angry, and I just wanted to hurt you. I got this stupid idea that sleeping with one of your friends was the only thing that would hurt you as much as you hurt me. Tom was there— he tried making excuses for you, but I wasn't interested in listening—but obviously he never would have done that to you. But Greg would do anything in a skirt, especially when he'd been drinking."

Fresh tears appeared in her eyes. "I'm sorry. As soon as I woke up the next morning and realized what I'd done I knew what a horrible mistake I'd made. I would have done anything to take it back. I still would. When Greg didn't seem to remember what happened, I was so relieved. I thought I could just pretend it didn't happen. I was the only one who seemed to know it had, and all I wanted to do was forget."

"And then you found out you were pregnant," Scott said.

Rachel swallowed hard. "Yes," she whispered roughly, the word barely audible.

"Why didn't you tell me?"

"I didn't know how. I was afraid you wouldn't forgive me. Would you have? *Can* you forgive me?"

Tellingly, painfully, he just stared at her, as though she was a stranger, not saying a word in response.

"What about me?" Greg asked coldly. "Aren't you going to ask for my forgiveness?"

Rachel looked at him in shock. "Is that why you're doing this? Why you killed Haley and Jess? Because I didn't tell you about the baby?"

"And Kim, don't forget her. I had to take care of her earlier because I knew you wouldn't invite her to the wedding. She's the one who told me what you'd done, what all of you had done. Part of her Twelve Steps, making amends to people she wronged. It didn't matter. She still had to pay. She still had to be punished. You all did. For conspiring to keep him a secret and give him away. Because you didn't wrong me, you wronged my son."

"He has a family, people who love him—"

"He's *dead*."

A hush fell over the room, the words seeming to echo endlessly in the stillness.

He's dead... He's dead... He's dead...

And that was when Meredith understood, Greg's words from the day before coming back to her.

Losing a child. That's not something any parent could get over...

Oh, God.

It didn't seem possible, but Rachel went even paler. "What are you talking about?"

"He died *two years ago!* Those people you gave him to, they had a pool. He fell in when they weren't looking and drowned before they even noticed. They didn't protect him. They let him die. So you are a murderer. As soon as you gave him to those people, you as good as killed him yourself!"

Rachel gave her head a desperate shake. "It was supposed to be better for him...."

"You mean better for *you.* You didn't even know, did you? You didn't even bother to keep track of him. You just gave him away and forgot all about him."

"No. I—I thought it would be easier not to know...."

"Well, it's not. I didn't know about him until it was too late, and it sure as hell isn't easier. I never got a chance to know him at all."

"What kind of father could you have been? You drank 24/7. And you really think that you could have been a parent, could have protected him? *You?*"

"I deserved to have the chance!"

Rather than deny it, Rachel simply closed her eyes, giving her head a small shake.

This was it. Meredith was finally close enough. She took a full step over, in front of Rachel.

Directly in front of the gun.

She watched Greg's eyes flare in outrage. "Move," he growled.

"No," she said, not letting herself react to the anger in his voice. "I'm not going to let you hurt her. You're going to have to shoot me first. And I don't believe you want to do that. You might have killed people you thought deserved it, but I don't think you believe I deserve that, do you, Greg?"

His mouth worked furiously, but he didn't say anything.

"And if you hurt Meredith in any way," Tom said with utter coldness, "then you're going to have to shoot me, too, before you can get to Rachel. Because I will be coming for you." His voice sounded closer, and she knew he must have moved nearer. Not close enough to intervene, but enough to truly have her back, exactly as promised.

"Me, too," Scott said. Out of the corner of her eye, she saw him finally, slowly, rise to his feet.

"And me," Rick said, his voice deadly calm.

"That's it, Greg," Meredith said. "If you want to kill Rachel, you're going to have to kill all of us first. Is it really worth it?"

From the frustrated rage on his face, he wanted to argue that it was. His eyes flicked from her to the others and back again, until resignation slowly fell over his features. "No," he murmured. "I guess it's not."

She felt no relief at hearing him say it. In spite of his words, he didn't lower his weapon, the gun remaining unwaveringly focused on her.

"So what now, Greg?" Tom asked calmly. "You've had your say. We all know the truth. Why don't you put the gun down?"

Greg looked down and past her, Meredith imagined, to where he could still see Rachel, even if he couldn't get a clear shot. "All right. Maybe it's better this way. Now you know your friends are dead because of you, the same way my son is. You have to live with that."

"And what about you?" Meredith asked softly. "What are you going to do?"

He shifted his eyes toward her, the look in them so chilling her heart leaped into her throat. He smiled. "I'm going to be with my son."

Before anyone could react he swung the gun to his own temple.

And pulled the trigger.

Meredith flinched, a scream bursting into her throat and sticking there, her tense muscles refusing to let it out. Instead, she could only stand there, trying to process what she'd just seen, trying to erase horror that had just unfolded before her. In the back of her mind she heard Rachel scream.

Then Tom was suddenly at her side, gently placing his hand on her elbow and leaning close. "Are you okay?"

She looked up into his eyes, taking in the concern on his face—and more important, the fact that he was whole and solid and unharmed. They both were. All of them—Scott, Rachel, Alex. Rick and Ellen.

It was finally over. They'd made it.

She managed a shaky nod. "Yes."

"Can you get everyone out of here? I'll check on Greg and get something to cover the body."

It took a second for the words to sink in. "We can close the room up until the police get here." Which didn't seem as urgent anymore. There was no longer a killer for them to apprehend, and the danger was over. No one else was going to be hurt.

At least, not physically, she amended, glancing over at Rachel and Scott. Rachel still sat in her chair. Scott stood in front of his. Several feet separated them, but they might as well have been a million miles apart. They didn't look at each other, didn't speak, simply remained where they were, shell-shocked.

Her heart aching for them, Meredith shook off her own remaining shock about what had happened. Squaring her shoulders, she moved forward. "Come on, you guys," she said gently but firmly, glancing toward Alex on the far side of the room to include him. "Let's get out of here."

The danger might be over, but these people were still

her guests, her responsibility, and they needed her, perhaps more than ever. Needed her to take charge, needed her to be there for them, needed her to be strong. And for their sakes, she would be.

As strong as she knew she could be.

Chapter Nineteen

"I think that should do it. You folks are free to go."

Tom felt a collective sigh of relief fill the study. The sheriff's pronouncement was what the wedding party had been waiting to hear for days. Now it was finally here.

After an endless night of waiting for the police to arrive, they'd finally made it through that morning. At long last, the bodies were taken away, the questions had been answered to the best of everyone's abilities and the remaining members of the wedding party were cleared to leave.

It was finally over.

Meredith rose to her feet. "Thank you, Sheriff. Let me walk you out."

With a nod to the rest of them, the sheriff followed her from the room.

Leaving the rest of them there, sitting in silence.

There were only four of them, Tom thought with a pang, surveying Scott, Rachel and Alex. When the cars carrying them had come up the mountain, they'd been full of passengers eager and excited for this weekend. Now it was time for the cars to make the return trip down the mountain, and there were only four left to take the journey.

Three, he amended. Because he wasn't going anywhere.

Alex was the first one to move, rising from his seat. "I

guess we should get moving then. I, for one, will be glad to get out of here."

Neither Rachel nor Scott disagreed with the statement. Neither of them said anything at all.

Rachel looked at Scott, her expression pained and pleading.

Scott stared straight ahead. He hadn't looked at her once since they'd entered the room.

Tom knew Scott hadn't spoken to her at all since yesterday. He'd jumped into the task of digging out from the storm, spending all afternoon and evening with Rick and Tom to uncover the rental cars and clear the driveway in front of the mansion so they'd be able to leave once the plow from town unblocked the road, Later he'd asked Meredith for a room of his own, then immediately headed to bed, exhausted like the rest of them. He'd claimed he was too busy to talk to Rachel. Tom suspected that as much as Scott wanted to get out of there, he'd also been making himself busy to avoid talking to her.

Something he still seemed determined to do. He finally stood, turning to face Alex. "Can you give Rachel a ride to the airport?"

Alex glanced between two of them, clearing his throat uncomfortably. "Uh, yeah, sure. I can do that."

Rachel burst to her feet, as well, evidently having had enough. "Scott, please. Talk to me."

He didn't even glance at her. "I don't think there's anything to say."

"I'm so sorry—"

"I know," Scott said simply, cutting her off. "It just doesn't change anything."

Rachel didn't seem to have a response to that, her face falling.

"Come on, Rach," Alex said, starting for the door. "Let's

get our bags and head to the airport. Maybe we can get home tonight."

With a resigned nod, she turned to follow him. When she reached the door, she stopped, placing her hand on it, and glanced back.

Scott kept his eyes steadfastly averted, his face hard as stone.

After a moment, she lowered her head and escaped into the hallway.

Almost immediately Scott seemed to relax, his shoulders sagging.

"You okay?" Tom asked him. He had a feeling he already knew the answer.

Scott gave a sharp shake of his head. "I just want to get out of here."

"You sure you don't want to talk to her?"

"There's no point. She lied about so much. She was going to marry me and there were so many things she'd kept from me. It's like I don't even know her. I don't know if I ever did." He looked at Tom. "What about you? You ready to head to the airport?"

That was the million-dollar question. And he definitely knew the answer.

"I don't think so," he said carefully. "I think I might stick around for a little while longer."

Scott's mouth curved slightly in a small, fleeting smile. "I had a feeling you might have some things to take care of here."

Tom grinned sheepishly. "Is it that obvious?"

"Pretty much. I've seen how you look at her, and how she looks at you." Scott bumped his fist on Tom's arm. "Good for you."

"Thanks. I admit it feels a little strange to have it happen in the middle of all this...."

"Hey," Scott said seriously. "Something good should come out of this. I'm happy for you."

Tom looked into his old friend's face, and beneath the weariness and sadness, he could tell Scott meant it. He wasn't so mysterious. He was Scott, the old friend he wanted to get to know again, the one he didn't want to lose touch with ever again.

They made their way out of the room and into the front hall. The front door was open, sunlight flooding through to fill the space. The sight was a little disconcerting. He'd never seen it so bright in here before. It looked completely different.

Then a figure came through the doorway, briefly blocking the light.

And there she was.

Meredith.

MEREDITH STOPPED JUST inside the door, her attention immediately drawn to the man standing at the base of the stairs.

Tom.

Her breath hitched at the sight of him.

You folks are free to go.

All of them.

He began to cross the space toward her. A nervous ripple quaking through her belly, she forced her feet to move to meet him.

They hadn't had much of a chance to talk in the past twenty-four hours. He'd been so busy digging out from the storm with Rick and Scott. He'd been gone all day, and at night he'd been exhausted. At least she'd had him in her bed. Even if he was too tired to talk, it was enough to have him there beside her, cradling her close. She hadn't let herself think about what would happen once the road was finally clear and the police came, wanting to cherish every moment she could.

But this was it. No putting it off any longer.

They met in the middle of the marble floor. He stopped a few feet in front of her. "Everyone's getting their bags to head to the airport."

What about you? she almost asked. Instead she glanced toward the stairs, where Scott had just disappeared at the top. "How's he doing?"

"Not great," he conceded. "But I think he'll be okay."

"Do you think there's any chance they'll work things out?"

He gave his head a small, sad shake. "I don't think they can. He told me it's like he doesn't even know her. She lied about so much."

With most of the others out of the house and Alex in his room, no doubt already beginning to write about the experience, Meredith had spent some time with Rachel yesterday. She knew what the other woman was going through. Greg had intended to devastate her life, and it seemed he'd succeeded. "She told me when they met again she thought she was being given a second chance to make things right."

"Unfortunately, I don't think she can."

It was sad, but Meredith could understand Scott's feelings. She knew what it was like to marry someone who wasn't who she'd thought he was. At least Scott had learned the truth before he'd taken those vows.

If only it hadn't come at such a high price…

"What about you?" Tom asked. "What's next for this place?"

"Adam and Jillian will be back this afternoon. And then I guess we'll decide what to do next."

"No more weddings?" he asked softly.

"Maybe Adam and Jillian's. I'm thinking a simple ceremony with no staff and no guests. Safer that way." She smiled sadly. "But otherwise, no. No more weddings."

"I'm sorry."

"It's all right," she said, not sure if she meant it. "I guess it wasn't meant to be."

He tilted his head back and took in the building. "This place is amazing, though. I'm sure you could find something to do with it. A hotel. A private retreat. Or…"

He trailed off, the suggestive lilt on that final words instantly grabbing her interest. "Or?"

"Or maybe you don't want to do anything with this place at all."

Her heart missed a beat, then quickly picked up speed. "Then what do I want to do?"

Tom met her eyes. "Maybe see what else is out there. See the world." He paused, his voice softening. "See how much more there can be. With me."

With him. There were so many ways to interpret those two little words, all of them wonderful.

And here it was, what she'd wanted for so long.

A new beginning.

Never in a million years would she have dreamed it would be with him.

She smiled, unable to keep the happiness off her face if she'd wanted to. "Is that an offer?"

He matched her smile, gracing her with that dazzling grin. "Is that a yes?"

She could have yelled it. Instead, she managed to nod, her smile widening as she said it.

"Yes."

She watched the joy dawn on his face. He lunged forward, his arms closing around her, lifting her up, pulling her close. She felt no tension at his touch, every bit of her melting against him. She knew this man's embrace. Nothing had ever felt like it. Nothing ever would.

He pulled back to look into her eyes. "I should point out that I don't have a job at the moment."

"Neither do I," she reminded him.

"When I get one, it could take me anywhere."

"Sounds great."

He grinned. "Want to see the world with me?"

The world, and so much more. "Absolutely."

The excitement on his face matching her own, he pressed his mouth to hers, then wrapped his arms around her.

It should have been terrifying. The uncertainty. The suddenness. The recklessness of it.

But it wasn't. It was a chance. The best one she'd ever been offered. She wasn't about to let it go.

Tom chuckled softly against her hair. "I have to admit, you're a lot different than I thought you were back in school."

Her heart stopped dead in her chest. Doing her best to hide her reaction, she eased her hold on him. This time she was the one who pulled back to look into his face. "What are you talking about? You didn't even know who I was in college."

His brows drew together, a quizzical look in his eye. "Sure I did. You used to draw those cartoons for the paper. I used to see you sitting in that quiet nook in the southeast corner of the quad, sketching on your pad."

Nothing he could have said would have surprised her more. All those years of thinking about him, she'd thought he had no idea she existed. She'd always thought she'd been invisible.

Somehow she found her voice. "Why didn't you ever say anything?"

He chuckled, lowering his head sheepishly. "Well, I have to admit, I always thought you were kind of intimidating."

She almost laughed in disbelief. "Me?"

"Sure. You seemed really intense. You were always so serious, always frowning. I can't remember ever seeing you smile."

That was because she hadn't, she reflected. She'd never thought she'd had a reason to.

She'd been protecting herself, guarding herself against the rejection of others by keeping them at bay.

Thinking of it now, she had to smile, nearly shaking her head. In disbelief. In amazement.

So much time wasted, for no better reason than she'd been afraid.

Taking in her expression, he grinned, too. "That's better."

And it was, she thought, her smile deepening, the warmth inside her growing as the realization, the certainty, washed over her.

She was done hiding. She was done being afraid.

She was ready for so much more.

Tom looked past her to the still-open door, the sunlight pouring in to fill the hall. "It feels like we've been in here forever, doesn't it? Do you want to go outside for a while?"

He was right. It was time to get out of here. "More than anything."

Releasing her, he stepped back and held out his hand.

That outstretched palm seemed to offer so much. A chance. A beginning. The world.

Her heart soaring, she placed her palm in his.

"Come on." With a laugh, he started forward, picking up speed, pulling her with him.

She quickly caught up, matching him step for step, as she raced him, laughing and smiling, into the light of a new day.

* * * * *

COMING NEXT MONTH from Harlequin® Intrigue®
AVAILABLE JUNE 18, 2013

#1431 OUTLAW LAWMAN

The Marshals of Maverick County

Delores Fossen

A search for a killer brings Marshal Harlan McKinney and investigative journalist Caitlyn Barnes face-to-face not only with their painful pasts but with a steamy attraction that just won't die. Only together can they defeat the murderer who lures them back to a Texas ranch for a midnight showdown.

#1432 THE SMOKY MOUNTAIN MIST

Bitterwood P.D.

Paula Graves

Who is trying to make heiress Rachel Davenport think she's going crazy? And why? Former bad boy Seth Hammond will put his life—and his heart—on the line to find out.

#1433 TRIGGERED

Covert Cowboys, Inc.

Elle James

When ex-cop Ben Harding is hired to protect a woman and her child, he must learn to trust in himself and his abilities to defend truth and justice...and allow himself to love again.

#1434 FEARLESS

Corcoran Team

HelenKay Dimon

Undercover operative Davis Weeks lost everything when he picked work over his personal life. But now he gets a second chance when Lara Barton, the woman he's always loved, turns to him for help.

#1435 CARRIE'S PROTECTOR

Rebecca York

Carrie Mitchell is terrified to find herself in the middle of a terrorist plot...and in the arms of her tough-guy bodyguard, Wyatt Hawk.

#1436 FOR THE BABY'S SAKE

Beverly Long

Detective Sawyer Montgomery needs testimony from Liz Mayfield's pregnant teenage client, who is unexpectedly missing. Can Sawyer and Liz find the teen in time to save her and her baby?

You can find more information on upcoming Harlequin® titles, free excerpts and more at www.Harlequin.com.

HICNM0613

REQUEST YOUR FREE BOOKS!
2 FREE NOVELS PLUS 2 FREE GIFTS!

HARLEQUIN®

INTRIGUE®

BREATHTAKING ROMANTIC SUSPENSE

YES! Please send me 2 FREE Harlequin Intrigue® novels and my 2 FREE gifts (gifts are worth about $10). After receiving them, if I don't wish to receive any more books, I can return the shipping statement marked "cancel." If I don't cancel, I will receive 6 brand-new novels every month and be billed just $4.74 per book in the U.S. or $5.24 per book in Canada. That's a savings of at least 14% off the cover price! It's quite a bargain! Shipping and handling is just 50¢ per book in the U.S. and 75¢ per book in Canada.* I understand that accepting the 2 free books and gifts places me under no obligation to buy anything. I can always return a shipment and cancel at any time. Even if I never buy another book, the two free books and gifts are mine to keep forever.

182/382 HDN F42N

Name _____ (PLEASE PRINT) _____

Address _____ Apt. # _____

City _____ State/Prov. _____ Zip/Postal Code _____

Signature (if under 18, a parent or guardian must sign) _____

Mail to the **Harlequin® Reader Service:**
IN U.S.A.: P.O. Box 1867, Buffalo, NY 14240-1867
IN CANADA: P.O. Box 609, Fort Erie, Ontario L2A 5X3

**Are you a subscriber to Harlequin Intrigue books
and want to receive the larger-print edition?
Call 1-800-873-8635 or visit www.ReaderService.com.**

* Terms and prices subject to change without notice. Prices do not include applicable taxes. Sales tax applicable in N.Y. Canadian residents will be charged applicable taxes. Offer not valid in Quebec. This offer is limited to one order per household. Not valid for current subscribers to Harlequin Intrigue books. All orders subject to credit approval. Credit or debit balances in a customer's account(s) may be offset by any other outstanding balance owed by or to the customer. Please allow 4 to 6 weeks for delivery. Offer available while quantities last.

Your Privacy—The Harlequin® Reader Service is committed to protecting your privacy. Our Privacy Policy is available online at www.ReaderService.com or upon request from the Harlequin Reader Service.

We make a portion of our mailing list available to reputable third parties that offer products we believe may interest you. If you prefer that we not exchange your name with third parties, or if you wish to clarify or modify your communication preferences, please visit us at www.ReaderService.com/consumerschoice or write to us at Harlequin Reader Service Preference Service, P.O. Box 9062, Buffalo, NY 14269. Include your complete name and address.

HI13R

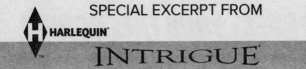

SPECIAL EXCERPT FROM

HARLEQUIN®

INTRIGUE®

Looking for another great Western read?
Jump into action with

TRIGGERED

by

Elle James

the first installment in the Covert Cowboys, Inc. series.

*When mysterious threats are made on the lives of
Kate Langsdon and her young daughter, only decorated
former Austin police officer Ben Harding is willing to
protect them at any cost.*

The warmth of his hands on her arms sent shivers throughout
her body. "Really, it's fine," she said, even as she let him
maneuver her to sit on the arm of the couch.

Ben squatted, pulled the tennis shoe off her foot and
removed her sock. "I had training as a first responder on the
Austin police force. Let me be the judge."

Kate held her breath as he lifted her foot and turned it to
inspect the ankle, his fingers grazing over her skin.

"See? Just bumped it. It'll be fine in a minute." She
cursed inwardly at her breathlessness. A man's hands on
her ankle shouldn't send her into a tailspin. Ben Harding
was a trained professional—touching a woman's ankle
meant nothing other than a concern for health and safety.
Nothing more.

Then why was she breathing like a teenager on her first
date? Kate bent to slide her foot back into her shoe, biting
hard on her lip to keep from crying out at the pain. When

she turned toward him she could feel the warmth of his breath fan across her cheek.

"You should put a little ice on that," he said, his tone as smooth as warm syrup.

Ice was exactly what she needed. To chill her natural reaction to a handsome man, paid to help and protect her, not touch, hold or kiss her.

Kate jumped up and moved away from Ben and his gentle fingers. "I should get back outside. No telling what Lily is up to."

Ben caught her arm as she passed him. "You felt it, too, didn't you?"

Kate fought the urge to lean into him and sniff the musky scent of male. Four years was a long time to go without a man. "I don't know what you're talking about."

Ben held her arm a moment longer, then let go. "You're right. We should check on Lily."

Kate hurried for the door. Just as she crossed the threshold into the south Texas sunshine, a frightened scream made her racing heart stop.

Don't miss the dramatic conclusion to
TRIGGERED by Elle James.

Available July 2013, only from Harlequin Intrigue.

SADDLE UP AND READ 'EM!

This summer, get your fix of Western reads and pick up a cowboy from the SUSPENSE category in July!

OUTLAW LAWMAN by Delores Fossen,
The Marshals of Maverick County
Harlequin Intrigue

TRIGGERED by Elle James,
Covert Cowboys, Inc.
Harlequin Intrigue

*Look for these great Western reads AND MORE,
available wherever books are sold or visit*
www.Harlequin.com/Westerns